She had never been touched so sensually

Sebastian grasped her chin, and something fierce sprang to life inside her the moment his mouth touched hers. He pushed her robe aside, his tanned fingers cupping the soft swell of one breast. Jessica pulled away.

"What's wrong?" he drawled. "Surely I took no liberties you've not permitted to countless others?"

The truth of the matter was, he had. "I'm not going to work for you," she told him quickly.

"You're trying to tell me you won't work for me because of this? If I haven't already made it clear, perhaps it's time I did. I'm not interested in other men's leavings. Don't mistake a timely warning for any desire for you, and that was all this was—a warning. You'll come with me—I promise you that."

PENNY JORDAN
is also the author of these

Harlequin Presents

These books may be available at your local bookseller.

For a free catalog listing all titles currently available,
send your name and address to:

HARLEQUIN READER SERVICE
1440 South Priest Drive, Tempe, AZ 85281
Canadian address: Stratford, Ontario N5A 6W2

PENNY JORDAN

passionate protection

Harlequin Books

TORONTO • NEW YORK • LONDON
AMSTERDAM • PARIS • SYDNEY • HAMBURG
STOCKHOLM • ATHENS • TOKYO • MILAN

Harlequin Presents first edition October 1983
ISBN 0-373-10633-5

Original hardcover edition published in 1983
by Mills & Boon Limited

CHAPTER ONE

'HONESTLY, Jess, I don't know what that family of yours would do without you,' Colin Weaver told his assistant with a wry smile. 'Well, what is it this time? Has your aunt locked herself out again, or your uncle forgotten to collect his new cheque book?'

'Neither,' Jessica Forbes told him, hiding her own smile. It was true that her aunt and uncle did tend to ring her at work for assistance every time there was a family crisis, but they weren't really used to the hectic pace of the modern-day commercial world—Uncle Frank, for instance, still lived in a pre-war daydream fostered by the leisurely pace of life in the small market town legal practice he had inherited from his father, and Aunt Alice wasn't much better; nervous, dithery, she was given to complaining in bewilderment that life had changed so much, she barely recognised it any more, and as for Isabel! Jessica sighed; the problems dumped on her by her eighteen-year-old cousin made those of her aunt and uncle seem mere nothings.

'Okay, okay, I'm sorry for criticising your beloved family,' Colin apologised with a wry smile. 'I suppose I'm just jealous really,' he admitted plaintively. 'Would you drop everything and come running for me if I locked myself out?'

'It wouldn't do any good if I did,' Jessica pointed out with a grin. 'You live in a penthouse

5

apartment, my aunt and uncle live in a rambling old vicarage with a pantry window that simply won't close, but which neither of them can fit through, whereas yours truly . . .'

'Umm, I'm beginning to get the point,' Colin agreed, glancing appreciatively over her slender five foot eight frame, 'but that doesn't stop me from wishing they would stop depriving me of your valuable assistance.'

'I have to go this time—it's Isabel.' Jessica frowned, chewing the soft fullness of her bottom lip, dark eyebrows drawn together in a worried frown. The problem was that her aunt and uncle had been slipping gently into middle age when Isabel had arrived unexpectedly on the scene and neither of them had ever totally recovered from the shock.

'Oh, Isabel,' Colin said grimly. 'That girl's lethal,' he added with a grimace. 'I remember when you brought her here . . .'

'Here' was his exclusive London salon where he showed the alluring ranges of separates that bore his name. Jessica had worked for him ever since she left art school. She loved her job as his assistant, and if he needed mollycoddling occasionally, he more than made up for his lapses when they were over. In Jessica's view there was no one to match him in the design of separates. His secret, he had told her on more than one occasion, lay as much in the careful choice of fabric as the style the materials were eventually made up in. 'Couture Classics' were how *Vogue* described them, and Jessica reckoned there could be few wealthy women in Britain aspiring to the well-dressed lists who didn't have something of his in their wardrobe. For some clients he designed individual ranges, but it was, as Jessica knew, his great dream to take his designs and elegance into the high streets at prices every woman could afford.

'She is a little immature,' Jessica agreed, repressing a sigh at the thought of her cousin— pretty, headstrong Isabel, who reminded her of a frisky lamb, throwing herself headlong into whatever came her way on a momentary whim.

'She's exactly two years younger than you were when you first came to work for me,' Colin reminded her a little grimly. 'You all keep that girl wrapped up in too much cotton wool, Jess, you spoil her, and she laps it up. What were you doing at eighteen? I bet you weren't still living at home, financed by Mummy and Daddy?'

'No,' Jessica agreed sombrely. Her parents had died three months before her eighteenth birthday. They had been killed in a car crash on their way home from visiting friends. She could still remember Uncle Frank trying to break the news; Aunt Alice's white face. They had offered her a home, of course, but by then she had her career planned, first art school and then, she hoped, a job in fashion design, and so instead she had used some of the money left to her by her parents and had bought herself a small flat in London, but she had stayed in close contact with her aunt and uncle; after all, they were the only family she had left, and as she grew older the ties between them had strengthened. Family came to mean a lot when there was so little of it left.

Isabel had been a little girl of ten at the time of the accident, too young to remember very much about Jessica's parents, and somehow Jessica had found that as the years went by she was called upon to mediate between impatient youth and dismayed late middle age in the storms that swept the household as Isabel grew into her teens, Isabel urging her to support her on the one hand, while her parents were pleading with Jessica to 'make Isabel realise' on the other.

The plan was that Isabel would go on to university after leaving school, but in the sixth form she had suddenly decided that she was tired of studying, that she didn't want a career at all, and so at eighteen she was working in her father's office, and complaining bitterly to Jessica about it whenever they met.

'I wanted to talk to you about our visit to Spain as well,' Colin said sulkily, interrupting her train of thought. Jessica gave him a teasing smile. At forty-eight he could sometimes display all the very worst characteristics of a little boy in the middle of a tantrum, and he was not above doing so to make her feel guilty or get her attention when he felt the need arise. Jessica excused him on the grounds that he was a first-rate designer and an excellent employer, flexible and with sufficient faith in her ability to make her job interesting. The Fabric Fair was something he had been dangling in front of her for several months. Initially he had planned to go alone, and then he had suggested that she should go with him. He heard by word of mouth about a Spanish firm who had discovered a series of new dyes for natural fibres, and that the results were stunningly spectacular. Their fabrics were sold only to the most exclusive firms, and Jessica knew that Colin was angling for an introduction to their Managing Director.

'I don't know whether I'll be able to go,' Jessica frowned, hiding a sudden shaft of amusement as his manner changed from smug satisfaction to anxious concern.

'Not that damn family of yours again!' he protested. 'This time you'll have to tell them to do without you. I need you, Jess,' he told her plaintively.

'Very well, but no more unkind comments about Isabel,' she reprimanded him severely. 'I know she's a little headstrong . . .'

'Headstrong! Stubborn as a mule would be a better description, but I can see nothing I have to say is going to have any effect on you, so you may as well finish early tonight.'

Colin really was a love, Jessica reflected fondly an hour later, opening the door to her flat. They had an excellent working relationship, and if she sometimes chafed against his avuncular manner it was a small price to pay for working with such a talented and experienced man. There was no one to follow him in the business, and he had already mentioned that he might be prepared to offer her a partnership if things went well. They would make a good team, he had told her, and Jessica agreed. In spite of his experience he would always listen to her suggestions, and often adopted them.

She grimaced at her reflection as she caught sight of it in the mirror. She had hurried away from the office without combing her hair or renewing her lipstick, and both looked untidy;

her lipstick because she constantly nibbled on her lower lip, and her hair from running impatient fingers through its sable length.

Without doubt her hair was her greatest asset, in her eyes; long, thick and glossy, it fell smoothly past her shoulders in a gentle bell. Sometimes she twisted it into an elegant chignon, on those days when Colin wanted her to meet clients and she wanted to create the right impression. One of the bonuses of working for a well known designer was the fact that she got most of her clothes at cost; another was that her lissom shape and long legs were ideally suited to the subtle tweeds, silks and linens Colin preferred to use.

'I do love seeing my clothes on a real woman,' he had told her once, appreciatively. 'Models are caricatures of the female species, clothes-horses, the complete antitheses of the heavy county types who buy from me, but you ... You might have been made for them,' he had told her.

Isabel laughed about her cousin's employer. 'An old woman' was how she referred to him, and while it had traces of truth, Jessica chided her. Colin was shrewd and extremely talented, and while he might not be as charismatic as many of the men Jessica came into contact with, he was genuine, with a genuine love for his chosen career.

Another thing Isabel derided was Jessica's own fastidious reluctance to indulge in what she was pleased to term 'fun'.

'Fun' to Isabel encompassed a wholly idealistic impression of what it was like living alone in London. In Jessica's place there was no end to the 'fun' she might have, but unlike Jessica, who was footloose and fancy-free, she was tied to the boring old parents, and dull Merton with its farmers and relaxed pace of life.

After one or two attempts to correct her misapprehensions Jessica had acknowledged that her cousin had no intention of letting herself be disillusioned, and besides, Jessica's 'freedom' was a useful tool to wield against her parents when rebellion stirred. It had struck Jessica more than once lately that her aunt and uncle were beginning to look tired. Uncle Frank was talking about retiring, and Jessica sensed that in some ways it would be a relief to them when Isabel eventually married and someone else took on the responsibility of their rebellious daughter. But so far Isabel had shown no signs of wanting to marry, and why should she? Jessica reflected. In her opinion eighteen was far too young—or perhaps that was just one of the penalties of still being single at twenty-six; one became super-cautious of marriage, of the risks and dangers involved in making such an enormous commitment to another human being, and demanding so much from them in return.

Jessica was aware that Isabel had a far lighter approach to life than she did herself and would consequently probably have a much easier ride through life. She sighed, and chided herself for getting old and cynical as she showered quickly, barely sparing the briefest glance at the slender length of her body before draping it in a towel and padding into her bedroom.

Jeans and a tee-shirt would suffice for the drive down to her aunt and uncle's, and she pulled them on quickly, zipping up the jeans before brushing her hair with a swift economy of movement. Her skin was good, thank goodness, and she rarely used much make-up; less when she was 'off duty'. Her eyes were a tawny gold—an unusual combination with the satin sable hair, oval and faintly Oriental, adding a dash of piquancy to her features, even if she did lack Isabel's pretty pouting beauty.

It was just after eight-thirty when she turned her small car into the familiar road leading to the Vicarage. She frowned as she remembered her aunt's tearful telephone call. What on earth had Isabel done this time?

Silence greeted her as she stopped the car and climbed out. Nine o'clock was normally supper time, so she walked round to the back of the house, knowing she would find her aunt in the kitchen.

Alice James gave a small start, followed by a relieved smile as she saw her niece, enveloping her in a warm hug.

'Jess! You made it—oh, I hoped you would! We've been so worried!'

'Is Belle here?' Jessica asked her, pulling a stool out from under the kitchen table and perching comfortably on it. She knew from old how long it took to drag a story out of her aunt.

'No. She's out, with . . . with John Wellington, he's the young partner your uncle's taken on. Belle seems pretty keen on him.'

'And that's a problem?' Jessica enquired humorously, correctly reading the note of doubt in her aunt's voice. 'I thought this was what you'd been praying for for the last couple of years—that she'd find someone safe and steady and settle down.' She was still at a loss to understand the reason for her aunt's concern. 'Isn't that what you've always wanted for her? A nice safe marriage?' she prompted again.

'Everything we wanted for her,' her aunt confirmed. 'And now it's all going to be spoiled, because of that wretched holiday!

'Holiday? What holiday?' Jessica asked, a frown creasing her forehead.

'Oh, it was several weeks ago. She wanted to go to Spain with a girl friend. John didn't want her to go—he's quite jealous—but you know what she's like. The very fact that he didn't only seemed to make her keener. Anyway, she went, and it was while she was there that it happened.'

'What happened?' Jessica asked patiently, quelling her rising dismay, her mind alive to all the fates that could befall a girl like her cousin, bent only on 'having a good time'.

'She got herself engaged—well, almost,' her aunt amended. 'To some Spanish boy she met over there. They've been writing to one another— none of us knew a thing about it, until she showed me his last letter. Jessica, what on earth are we going to do? She's as good as promised to marry John, and if he finds out about this . . .'

'Why should he?' Jessica asked practically, mentally cursing Isabel. Trust her to have two men dangling; she was all for the competitive spirit, Jessica acknowledged wryly. 'All she has to do is to write to this Spanish boy and simply tell him that it's over.' Privately she was surprised that Isabel's Spaniard had bothered to write; most of them made a hobby out of 'falling in love' with pretty tourists.

'She daren't. She's terrified that he'll come over here to find out what's happening, and then what on earth will she tell John?'

If Isabel didn't feel able to tell John the plain truth now, it didn't bode well for their marriage, was Jessica's private opinion, but she refrained from voicing it, practically deciding that her aunt's obvious distress was what needed her attention right now.

'Don't worry about it,' she soothed her. 'It will all be all right.'

'Oh, Jess, I knew you'd be able to sort it all out,' her aunt confided, promptly bursting into tears. 'I told Isabel you'd help.'

Jessica spread her hands ruefully. 'Of course, but I don't see what I can do . . .'

'Why, go to Spain, of course,' her aunt announced as though she were talking about a trip to the nearest town. 'You must go and see him, Jess, and explain that Isabel can't marry him.'

'Go to Spain?' Jessica stared at her. 'But, Aunt . . .'

'You were going anyway,' her aunt said hurriedly, avoiding her eyes, 'and you can speak Spanish, Jessica, you can explain to him in his own tongue, soften the blow a little. Think what it would do to Isabel if he were to come here. She genuinely cares for John, and I think he has the strength she needs.' She sighed. 'I sometimes think your uncle and I should have been stricter with her, but . . .' she broke off as the kitchen door suddenly burst open and a small, fair-haired girl hurried in. She stopped dead as she reached the table.

'Jess!' she exclaimed joyfully. 'Oh, you've come—thank goodness! Has Mum told you . . .'

'That you're being pursued by an ardent suitor? Yes,' Jessica told her cousin dryly. 'Honestly, Belle . . .'

'I really thought I loved him,' Isabel began defensively. 'He was so different from John, and it was all so romantic . . . Oh, there's no need to look like that!' She stamped her foot as Jessica raised her eyes heavenwards. 'It's different for you, Jess, you'd never get involved in anything like that, you're so sensible, so unromantic, but me . .'

Jessica winced a little as her cousin's unthinking comment found its mark. How often had she heard that comment 'You're so unromantic'? Every time she refused to go to bed with her escort? Every time she refused to get involved? And yet she had always thought secretly that she was too romantic; that her ideals were too high.

'You're really sure then about John?' Jessica questioned her cousin later in the evening when they were both preparing for bed.

'As sure as I'm ever likely to be,' Isabel told her with a rare flash of honesty. 'But it will spoil everything if Jorge decides to come over here to find out why I've stopped writing to him. You will go and see him, won't you, Jess?' she appealed. 'I don't think I could bear it if I lost John!'

There were tears in her eyes, and unwillingly Jessica felt herself giving way. She supposed it wouldn't hurt to try and see this boy while she was in Spain; even perhaps add a few days to the trip to make sure she did see him, although she was quite convinced that it was highly unlikely that he would turn up in England.

'But you don't understand,' Isabel wailed when she pointed this out to her. 'We were practically engaged. He will come over, Jess, I know he will!' She practically wrung her hands together in her fear, and Jessica, feeling immeasurably more than only eight years her senior, sighed.

'Well, I'll go and see him then, but honestly, Belle, I'm sure you're worrying unnecessarily.'

'You mean to tell me you actually agreed to go and see this impetuous Romeo on your cousin's behalf?' Colin expostulated three days later when she explained to him that she would like to add a couple of extra days' holiday to their trip to Spain. 'Can't she do her own dirty work?'

'Not in this case,' Jessica assured him, quickly outlining the facts. 'And of course, I do speak Spanish.'

In actual fact she spoke several foreign languages. They were her hobby and she seemed to have a flair for them.

'Well, I can see that nothing I can say is going to cure you of this protective attitude towards your family,' Colin admitted. 'All I can say is— thank goodness I don't have one!'

'And my extra days' holiday?'

'They're yours,' he agreed. 'Although I'd much rather see you spend them on yourself than squander them on young Isabel. She's a leech, Jess, and she'll suck you dry if you let her. You must see that, so why?'

'She's family,' Jessica said simply. 'She and my aunt and uncle are all I have left.'

Often she had wondered after her parents' shocking deaths if the accident had somehow not only robbed her of her mother and father, but her ability to love as well, because ever since then she had held the world at a distance, almost as though she was afraid of letting people get too close to her; afraid that she might come to depend on them and that she would ultimately lose them.

Seville was a city that appealed strongly to the senses. Jessica fell in love with it almost from the moment she stepped off the plane into the benevolent spring sunshine. Madrid was more properly the home of Spanish commerce, and Jessica had been there on several previous occasions, but Seville was new territory to her.

Initially she had been surprised when Isabel told her that Jorge lived in Seville; she had expected to find him somewhere on the Costa Brava, but Isabel had told her that Jorge had been holidaying like herself at the time they met.

Colin, running true to form, had insisted on her staying at the hotel the extra few days at his expense, and although Jessica had demurred, he had insisted, and in the end she had given way. Knowing Colin, the hotel he would have chosen would be far more luxurious than anything she could have afforded, and this supposition was proved correct when her taxi drew up outside an impressive Baroque building.

Her fluent Spanish brought a swift smile to the face of the girl behind the reception desk, and in no time at all she was stepping out of the lift behind the porter carrying her case and waiting while he unlocked the door to her room.

The hotel had obviously once been a huge private house, and had been converted tastefully and carefully. Jessica's room had views over the city; the furniture, although reproduction, was beautifully made and totally in keeping with the age and character of the room. There was a bathroom off it, rather more opulent than she would have expected in the hotel's British equivalent, a swift reminder that this part of the world had once been ruled by the Moors, who had left behind them a love of luxury and a sensuality that had been passed down through the generations.

Once she had unpacked Jessica went down to the foyer, where she had seen some guide books and maps on sale. The evening meal, as she was already aware, was the all-important meal in the Spanish home, and she wanted to make sure that her visit to Jorge did not clash with this.

As she had suspected, the receptionist was able to confirm that in Seville it was the general rule to eat later in the evening—normally about ten o'clock—which gave her the remainder of the afternoon and the early evening to make her visit, Jessica decided.

She had already formulated a plan of action. First she intended to discover if Jorge's family were listed in the telephone directory. If they were she would telephone and ask when she might call, if not she would simply have to call unannounced.

She lunched lightly in the hotel's restaurant— soup, followed by prawn salad, and then went up to her room to study the telephone directory. There were several Calvadores listed in the book, but none under Jorge's address, and Jessica was forced to the reluctant conclusion that she would simply have to call unannounced.

A call to the reception desk organised a taxi to take her to her destination. She showered and changed into soft jade green silk separates, from Colin's new range; a pleated skirt that swirled softly round her legs and a blouson top with full sleeves caught up in tight cuffs. The colour suited her, Jessica knew, and to complement it she brushed toning jade eye-shadow over her lids, thickening and darkening her lashes discreetly with mascara.

Soft kid sandals of jade, blue and cerise completed her outfit. It was warm enough for her to be able to dispense with a jacket, and she was just flicking a comb through the silken length of her hair when her phone buzzed and the receptionist announced that her taxi had arrived.

Because she spoke Spanish so well, Jessica had no qualms about giving the driver instructions herself, but she began to wonder if, after all, she had made some mistake, when they drove into what was obviously a very luxurious and exclusive part of the city. Imposing buildings lined the streets, here and there an iron grille giving a tantalising view of the gardens beyond. Fretworked balconies and shutters lured the eye, but Jessica was left with an overall impression of solitude and privacy strictly guarded, so that it was almost as though the buildings themselves seemed to resent her intrusion.

At last the taxi stopped, and rather hesitantly she asked him if he could return for her in half an hour. That surely would give her sufficient time to explain the situation to Jorge? She only prayed that he was in!

Quickly checking the address Isabel had written down on the scrap of paper she had given her, she climbed unsteadily out of the car and glanced hesitantly at the imposing frontage of the building. There was no need for her to feel nervous, she reassured herself; the building, impressive though its outward appearance was, probably housed dozens of small apartments. However, when she reached the top of the small flight of stone steps there was simply one bell. She pressed it and heard the faint ringing somewhere deep in the recesses of the building. An aeon seemed to pass before she heard sounds of movement behind the large studded door.

Honestly, it was almost like something out of a horror movie! she reflected as the door swung back, creaking on its hinges.

The man who stood there had 'upper class servant' stamped all over his impassive countenance. He looked disapprovingly at Jessica for several seconds and appeared to be on the point of closing the door in her face when she babbled quickly, 'My name is Jessica James and I've come to see Señor Calvadores. Is he at home?'

The man seemed to consider her for an age before grudgingly opening the door wide enough for her to step into a hallway large enough to hold her entire flat. The floor was tiled with the famous *azulejo* tiles, so beautiful that she almost caught her breath in pleasure. If only Colin could see these! The colours were fantastic, shading from softest blue to a rich deep azure.

'If the *señorita* will please wait,' the manservant

murmured, opening another door and indicating that Jessica was to precede him into the room. Like the hall, it was enormous, furnished in what she felt sure must be priceless antiques. Whoever Jorge was, he quite obviously was not a poor man, she reflected, gazing in awe at her surroundings.

'Señorita James?' he repeated slowly. 'I will see if *el Señor Conde* can see you.'

'*El Señor Conde!*' Jessica stared after his departing back. Isabel had said nothing to her about a title. What was the matter with her? she asked herself sardonically several seconds later; surely she wasn't impressed by something as outmoded as an inherited title? She, who had always despised those who fawned on the county and titled set, because of who they were rather than what they were!

She was lost in a deep study of a portrait above the fireplace—a Spanish don of the seventeenth century if she was any judge, formidable and with a magnetism that refused to be confined to the canvas—when she heard footsteps outside the door, firmer and far more decisive than the man-servant's. She felt herself tense. Now that the moment was almost upon her she felt ridiculously nervous. What on earth was she going to say? How could she simply say baldly that Isabel no longer wanted him; and that in fact he was an embarrassment to her, now that she was on the verge of becoming engaged to another man.

The door opened and the man who stood there took her breath away. Her first impression was that he was impossibly arrogant, standing there staring down the length of his aristocratic nose at her, his lean jaw tensing, as though he was controlling a fierce anger. Ice-cold grey eyes flicked disparagingly over her, the aquiline profile inclining slightly in an acknowledgement of her presence, which was more of an insult than a courtesy.

He was tall, far taller than she had expected, his hair dark, sleek as raven's feathers, and worn slightly long, curling over the pure silk collar of a shirt she was sure had been handmade especially for him.

Everything about this man whispered discreetly of wealth and prestige, and never in a million years could Jessica imagine him holidaying on the Costa Brava and indulging in a holiday romance with her cousin.

For one thing, he must be almost twice Isabel's age—certainly in his early thirties—and nothing about him suggested the type of man who needed the admiration of a very young girl to boost his ego. This man did not need any woman; his very stance suggested an arrogant pride which would never admit to any need of any kind. He was the result of centuries of wealth and breeding of a type found almost exclusively in the great Spanish families, and Jessica felt her blood run cold at the thought of telling him that her cousin had decided she preferred someone else.

'Señorita James?'

He spoke perfect accentless English, his voice clipped and cool, and yet despite his outward control, Jessica sensed that beneath the ice-cold surface raged a molten torrent of barely held in rage. But why? Or had he guessed her purpose in coming? This man was no fool, surely he must have realised from the recent tone of Isabel's letters how the land lay?

'Señor Calvadores?'

Her voice was no way as controlled as his, and she had the dismal conviction that he knew he had unnerved her and that he deliberately intended to.

It was obvious that he didn't intend to make things easy for her. So much for Spanish hospitality! Jessica thought indignantly. He hadn't even offered her so much as a cup of coffee. Well, there was nothing for it but to plunge in; there was no easy way to say what had to be said, and all she wanted to do now was to say her piece and make her escape. His attitude and hauteur had killed all the sympathy she had initially felt towards him. Never in a thousand years could she imagine her flighty young cousin holding her own against this man whose very stance exuded an arrogant contempt that filled the air around them.

'I've come to see you about . . .'

'I know what you've come to see me about, Miss James,' he cut in brutally, not allowing her to finish, 'and no doubt you want me to make things easy for you. No doubt you hoped to sway me with your large, worried eyes, no doubt you've been led to believe that I can be persuaded to give way. Unfortunately—for you—that is not to be. To put it in its simplest form, Miss James, and having seen you for myself, having had confirmed every one of my very worst fears—that is to say, having seen for myself that you are a young woman who likes expensive clothes, and doubtless everything that goes with them; that you are at a guess somewhere in your mid-twenties; that you are bold enough to come here demanding to see me; there is simply no way I shall allow you to ruin my brother's life by trapping him into marriage simply because of an affair you had with him several months ago!'

Jessica was totally lost for words. His brother, he had said. That meant he wasn't—couldn't be Jorge de Calvadores, but he obviously thought she was Isabel. She was on the verge of correcting him when she realised what else he had said. 'An affair'. Isabel had said nothing about an affair to her; indeed, Isabel had given her the distinct impression that Jorge was the one pressing her into an unwanted engagement, whereas his brother seemed to think the boot was very much on the other foot. Clearly there were some misunderstandings to be sorted out!

CHAPTER TWO

SHE took a deep breath, wondering where to begin. Perhaps if she were to explain to him first that she wasn't Isabel. How contemptuous he had been about her cousin! He really was insufferably proud and arrogant; she didn't like him at all, she decided, eyeing him militantly.

She opened her mouth to explain, but was stunned into silence by the cynical way he was looking at her; a way no man had ever looked at her before, she realised, feeling the heat rising through her body. His study was an openly sexual one, and not merely sexual but contemptuous. Good heavens, it could have been Isabel exposed to that merciless scrutiny that made no allowance for feminine modesty or embarrassment! And she had thought Spaniards were supposed to be reticent, cultured and, above all, respectful to women!

'You don't understand,' she began shakily when she had recovered her composure, anger fanned into tiny, darting flames by the look she had seen in his eyes.

'On the contrary, I understand all too well,' came the crisp response. '*Dios*, do you not think I know what goes on at these holiday resorts?' His finely cut mouth curled sneeringly downwards. 'You must have thought yourself extremely fortunate to meet a young man as wealthy and unworldly as my young brother, but unfortunately for you, Jorge does not come into his inheritance for half a dozen more years, when he reaches his twenty-fifth birthday. Until then I stand guardian to him, and you may take it that I shall do everything in my power to free him from your clutches. I must say I am surprised at your coming here,' he added. 'I thought Jorge had already made it clear to you that the affair was over. You should have persuaded him to pay for his pleasure at the time, Miss James,' he told her contemptuously. 'Now it is too late; now he sees you for what you really are.' His lip curled, and Jessica went hot and cold to think of Isabel being forced to stand here and listen to these insults.

'Your brother loved m-my ... me,' she corrected herself hurriedly. 'He ...'

'—Desired your body,' she was told flatly, 'and in his innocence mistook such desire for a far different emotion—a fact which you used to your advantage, using his lust for you to force him ...'

'Just a moment!' she inserted, with a sudden resurgence of her normal coolness. 'If you are implying that Jorge was forced into ...'

'Oh, I am aware that there was no question of "force" as such,' the icy voice agreed. 'Bemused, dazzled, dragged out of his depth—these would perhaps be better descriptions. You are an attractive woman,' he told her, openly assessing the shape of her body beneath the thin silk, 'not perhaps in Jorge's usual style, but no matter ... Of course I realise why you are here. I suppose you thought that a personal appearance might be just the goad he needed. Absence makes the heart grow fonder—of someone else, is that it?'

Matters had gone far enough. There was a

limit to the amount of time she intended to simply stand there and allow him to insult her.

'Before we go any further, I ought to tell you that I have no desire at all to become engaged to your brother,' Jessica told him truthfully, 'In fact...'

'Oh, come, you cannot expect me to believe that?' he said softly. 'Perhaps I should refresh your memory. I have here your last letter to Jorge. He brought it to me in a very troubled frame of mind. It seems that while he enjoyed your... company, the constant pressure you put on him to announce your engagement has panicked him into confiding in me.'

'You having considerable experience of ridding yourself of unwanted women, I suppose?' Jessica supplied sweetly. 'One of the penalties of being wealthy!'

The dark flush of colour beneath his skin brought her a fierce sense of satisfaction. He hadn't liked her implication that women would only find him attractive for his wealth, and she knew it wasn't true. He was too intensely male for that. She found herself wondering if he was married, and then squashed the thought as being of no concern to her.

'You must accept that Jorge no longer wishes to have anything to do with you,' she was told implacably, 'and even if he did, I would do everything in my power to dissuade him from marrying a woman like you. What attracted you to him the most? Or can I guess?'

'If you did you'd be wrong,' Jessica told him in a clipped voice. 'As I've already said, I have no desire to marry your brother.'

'No?' With a swift movement he reached inside his jacket and removed a folded piece of paper. 'Read this—perhaps it will help you remember,' he said contemptuously.

Unwillingly Jessica took the letter, her fingertips brushing his as she did, strange quivers of sensation running up her arm as she recoiled from the brief contact.

Matters had gone far enough. She would have to tell him the truth. She opened the letter, and her heart dropped. She had barely done more than read the first couple of lines, skimming quickly over them, but it was enough to bring a burning colour to her face. Isabel and Jorge had been lovers—that much was obvious; as was Isabel's impassioned plea for Jorge to marry her. What on earth had possessed her cousin to write a letter like this? Jessica felt sick at the thought of her aunt and uncle reading it; and what about John? Why on earth hadn't Isabel warned her? And why had she been so convinced that Jorge intended to come to England? To judge from his brother, the young Spaniard wanted to escape from the relationship just as much as Isabel herself.

'Edifying, is it not?' her persecutor drawled insultingly. 'And I understand from Jorge—although he was reluctant to admit it—that he was far from being your first lover.'

Jessica's eyes widened, mirroring her shock. Was it true?

'So, obviously realising that your letter had failed, you decided to come in person. Why, I wonder? It must surely be obvious to you by now that Jorge does not wish to marry you.'

What on earth had Isabel got her into?

For a moment she contemplated telling the truth, but to do so meant betraying her cousin. She had protected Isabel for too long to stop now.

'Perhaps, failing marriage, you had something else in mind?' The soft suggestion held a trace of bitter contempt. 'I know Jorge has told you of the marriage his family had hoped might take place between him and the daughter of a close friend of ours—a marriage, I might add, which would stand a far greater chance of success than the one you proposed. Perhaps you hoped to turn this fact to your advantage. Barbara's family are very old-fashioned. They would be intolerant of any folly on Jorge's part.'

Jessica went white, reaching out blindly to grasp the back of a chair for support as the meaning of his words sank in.

'You thought I'd use blackmail!' she whispered disbelievingly. 'You thought I came here to . . . to . . .'

'Very affecting,' the cool voice mocked. 'But I am not Jorge, to be easily impressed by a pair of huge amber eyes that plead with me to believe in an innocence I know they cannot possess. You are several years older than my brother; you used his inexperience and calf-love for you to further your own ends. You must have known that his family would never tolerate such an alliance—so, Miss James, let us get down to business, shall we?'

'If by business you mean you'll pay me to forget any claims I might have on your brother, you're wasting your time!' Jessica told him furiously, too angry to care about the danger emanating from him as she pushed bitterly past him, blinking away tears of rage as she wrestled with the huge front door. She could hear him behind her, and the terrible fear that he would never allow her to leave made the blood pound in her head, her fingers trembling as she tugged at the door.

He swore harshly and she felt his hand on her shoulder, sobbing with relief as the door yielded and she half stumbled into the street. Her taxi was waiting and she flung herself into it without a backward glance, not caring what conclusions her driver might be drawing. The first thing she intended to do when she got back to the hotel was to put a call through to her cousin and find out exactly what was going on.

Fortunately, it was her aunt and uncle's bridge night, and Isabel answered the phone, her pleasure turning to petulance as she recognised the anger in Jessica's voice.

'You saw Sebastian?' she exclaimed nervously. 'Oh, no, Jess, what did he say?'

She had a good mind to tell her, Jessica thought wrathfully. So Sebastian was his name; it suited him somehow.

'Nothing flattering,' she assured Isabel grimly. 'In fact he seemed to think I was you. Oh, Belle,' she exclaimed as the scene in the vast and opulent drawing room flashed quickly through her mind, 'you should have warned me, told me the truth. Why on earth did you want me to come here? Sebastian told me that Jorge had no desire to become engaged to you, he even showed me your letter.'

She knew from the sudden catch in her breath

that Isabel hadn't expected that, and yet true to
form her cousin, even now, seemed to be trying
to turn the situation to her own advantage.

'You didn't tell him he was wrong, did you?'
she asked quickly, 'about us, I mean, Jess?'

'I wasn't given the opportunity,' Jessica told
her dryly. It hadn't been pleasant listening to
what the arrogant Conde had to say, and some of
his more stinging barbs still hurt.

'He mustn't know,' Isabel was saying positively. 'Oh, Jess, try to understand—when I
wrote that letter to Jorge, I was desperate—I
thought I might be pregnant . . . Jess . . . Jess, are
you still there?'

Trying not to betray her shock, Jessica
murmured an assent. 'Oh, you don't understand
at all,' she heard Isabel saying crossly, obviously
correctly interpreting her silence. 'Honestly, Jess,
you're so old-fashioned it just isn't true! Living
like a frigid spinster might suit you, but it doesn't
suit me,' she told her frankly, 'and why shouldn't
I have fun if I want to?'

'Was it fun, thinking you might be pregnant
and unmarried?' Jessica asked her bluntly. Isabel
was still very much a spoiled child, and it did
neither of them any good thinking now that she
should have been treated far more firmly as a
child—the damage was done, and Isabel seemed
to think she had a God-given right to indulge
herself in whatever she chose.

'No,' she heard Isabel admit sulkily. 'But what
else could I do? I had to write to him—he was as
responsible as me.'

'Go on,' Jessica told her briefly. The more she
heard, the less able she felt to defend her

cousin—but then there were her aunt and uncle to think of. Both of them would be unbearably shocked if they heard the truth.

'Oh, nothing.' She could almost see Isabel's petulant shrug. 'I discovered it was a false alarm, by that time I had met John, and so . . .'

'So you asked me to come here to see someone I thought you were on the verge of becoming engaged to. I don't understand, Belle. There must be something more to it.'

There was a long silence during which mingled exasperation and fear gripped her, and then at last Isabel admitted sulkily,

'Oh, all right then, when I wrote to Jorge he didn't write back, but his brother did. Jorge had shown him my letter, he said, and he wanted to know what proof there was that any child I might have was Jorge's—beast!' she added vitriolically. 'It was a hateful letter, Jess, and I was scared— Jorge had told me about him, that he was his guardian and that he was very strict. I was terrified he might come over here—come and see me because of what I'd written—so I panicked. I thought if you could see Jorge and tell him that I didn't want him any more then he would tell Sebastian and . . .'

And she would have been safe, without having to endure the unpleasantness of an interview with either Jorge or Sebastian, Jessica reflected bitterly. Trust Isabel to want to wriggle out of the situation with the minimum amount of discomfort to herself!

'You do understand, don't you, Jess?' Isabel pleaded. 'I couldn't run the risk of Sebastian coming over here. If the parents or John had seen him . . .'

'So you sent me into the lion's den instead,' Jessica supplied dryly. 'Thanks!'

'I didn't know that you'd see Sebastian or that he'd mistake you for me,' Isabel defended herself, 'but perhaps it's all worked out for the best,' she added with what to Jessica was colossal selfishness. 'Now he's seen you and you've told him that you don't want Jorge, he won't bother us again. What was he like?' she asked curiously. 'To hear Jorge talk about him anyone would think he was God!' She giggled. 'I quite fancied meeting him; Jorge said all the women were after him. He's immensely wealthy, and the title goes back to the days of Ferdinand and Isabella. He sounded fearfully haughty and proud.'

It was becoming obvious that Isabel knew far more about the Calvadores family than she had told her, Jessica realised. She was furious with her cousin, but as she knew from past experience, it was pointless getting angry with Isabel. Even if she were to drag her out here and make her face Sebastian and Calvadores herself, what possible good could it do? Isabel was probably right, it had all turned out for the best, although Jessica doubted that he would ever have felt sufficient concern about her hold over his brother to go the lengths of seeking her out in England.

'He sent me the most hateful letter,' Isabel was saying, her voice quivering slightly. 'He said that he didn't believe I might be pregnant and that it was just a trick to get Jorge to marry me. At least it's all over with now, Jess,' she added on a happier note, 'I'm so relieved. By the way,' she added coquettishly, 'John proposed last night and I've accepted him—the parents are over the moon!'

Privately Isabel thought her cousin far too young to be thinking of marriage. It was plain that Isabel was far from mature, and she doubted that John was the right husband for her, but she knew better than to interfere.

'When will you be back?' Isabel demanded. 'We're having a proper engagement party, and I want you to be there, of course.'

A sop to ease her conscience, Jessica thought wryly. She had done the dirty deed for her and now she was to be rewarded; Isabel couldn't get engaged without her. Had her cousin the slightest idea of what it had felt like to have to stand there and listen to Sebastian de Calvadores' insults? To be told that her morals were questionable, that she was motivated by financial greed—no, she thought grimly, Isabel didn't have the slightest conception.

Since she had allowed herself two days to sort out Isabel's romantic problems, Jessica found herself with a day on her hands. She wasn't going to waste it, she decided as she breakfasted in her room on warm rolls and fresh honey. She would explore Seville.

She already knew a little about it; that it had once been ruled by the Moors who had ruled all this part of Spain; that during the Middle Ages it had had a fine reputation as a centre of medical learning. Once Colin arrived there would be scant time for sightseeing, which in any case did not interest him, so after checking the time of his flight, which was due in early in the evening, Jessica collected her guide books and set out to explore the city.

But as she wandered the Moorish Alcazar,

instead of simply being able to drink in its beauty, at almost every turn she was forcibly reminded of Sebastian de Calvadores; it was from the men who had built the civilisation from which this beauty had sprung that he drew his arrogance, she thought as she looked around her. There was Moorish blood running in his veins, underlining and emphasising his total masculinity. She shivered, suddenly feeling cold, glad to step out into the warmth of the sunshine. Forget him, she told herself, why worry about what had happened? She knew that he had been totally mistaken about it, and that should have been enough. But somehow it wasn't. She could forget the contempt in his eyes, the explicitly sexual way they had moved over her body and yet at the same time had remained so cold, as though he had been saying, see, I know everything there is to know about you as a woman and it does nothing for me, nothing at all.

If it wasn't for the fact that by doing so she would betray Isabel she would have gone back and told him how wrong he was about her; then it would be his turn to feel her contempt, her condemnation.

Seville was a beautiful city, but she wasn't in the mood to enjoy it. Almost everywhere she looked she was reminded of Sebastian de Calvadores; Moorish faces, sternly oppressive, stared back at her from paintings; Moorish men who had guarded their women like precious jewels in rare caskets and who would never in a million years permit them the kind of freedom Isabel enjoyed.

Chastity and desire burned strongly in twin

flames in these people; either saints or sinners, but knowing no middle road; their history was a proud one and there could be few natives of Seville who did not boast some Moorish blood, some fierce elemental strain they had inherited from their forebears. They had been a race who, even while they tasted the cup of pleasure to the full, always remained a little aloof, knowing that where there was pleasure there was pain. A cynical, sophisticated race who had kept their women closeted away from the world to be enjoyed by them alone.

Jessica was glad when the time came to go and meet Colin's plane. He seemed so solid and safe somehow as he came towards her, carrying his briefcase, frowning uncertainly until he saw her.

'Jessica!' His hug was affectionately warm. 'Everything sorted out?' he asked her as they got into their taxi, his tone implying that he wouldn't be surprised to find that Isabel in her tiresomeness had allowed her problems to overflow into Jessica's working life.

'I think so.'

His relief made her laugh. 'Thank goodness for that! I was terrified that we'd have a tearful besotted Latin lover on our hands!'

Just for a moment Jessica compared this image to the reality of Sebastian, and wondered if Jorge was anything like his formidable brother. Probably not. She couldn't see Sebastian allowing himself to be manipulated in the way she was coming to suspect that Isabel had manipulated Jorge. No, when it came to the woman in his life, Sebastian would be totally in control. Was he married?

'Jess?'

Stop thinking about him, she chided herself, giving her attention to Colin. She was in Seville to work, not concern herself with the private life of a man who was virtually a stranger. Stranger or not, for those first few pulsating seconds when she had seen Sebastian she had been aware of him in a way that still had the power to shock her. For all his repressive arrogance there was a sensuality about him, a total maleness and a dangerous allure, reminiscent of that of a jungle cat for its prey.

Colin was tired after his flight and it was decided that he would dine in his room and have an early night.

'Have you been to the exhibition centre yet?' he asked Jessica. She shook her head. 'Well, the exhibition doesn't open until tomorrow. We've got an appointment with Calvortex after lunch. Keep your fingers crossed, won't you?' he asked her. 'I've done all next season's designs with their fabrics in mind. If they're anything like last season's we'll be on to a real winner—especially if he gives us the exclusive use of his stuff for the U.K.'

'How much do you know about them?' Jessica asked him as they stepped into the hotel foyer.

'Very little, and most of that word of mouth. The Chairman of the company handpicks his clients, from what I've been told. The company is a small family-run business; apart from that I know nothing, except that they produce the sort of fabrics that fill the dreams of every designer worth his or her salt. I'm relieved to hear you've sorted out all that business with Isabel,' he added as they headed for the lift. 'Tiresome girl! Why should you run round after her?'

'Well, I won't have to much longer,' Jessica told him. 'She's got herself engaged.'

'God help the man!' was Colin's pious comment as the lift stopped at their floor.

Their rooms were not adjacent and outside the lift they went their separate ways.

In her own room, Jessica tried to concentrate on the morning and the textile show, but somehow Sebastian de Calvadores' aquiline features kept coming between her and her work. A hard man and a proud one, and her face burned with colour as she remembered the way he had looked at her, the insulting remarks he had made to her.

She went to bed early, and was just on the point of falling asleep when she heard someone knocking on the door.

'Jess, are you awake?' she heard Colin mutter outside. 'I've got the most dreadful indigestion, do you have anything I can take?'

Sighing, she went to her suitcase and found some tablets. If Colin had one fault it was that he was a hopeless hypochondriac and that he refused absolutely to carry even aspirins about with him, preferring instead to play the martyr for the uninitiated. Jessica had got wise to this within her first few months of working from him, and had grown used to carrying what amounted almost to a small pharmacy around with her whenever she travelled with him.

She opened her door and handed him the small packet.

'You're an angel!'

Colin bent forward, kissing her cheek lightly, and as he did so out of the corner of her eye Jessica glimpsed the couple walking down the corridor towards them; the woman small and petite with smoothly coiled dark hair and an expensive couture evening gown, her escort tall, with raven's-wing dark hair and a profile that made Jessica's heart turn over thuddingly as she stared at him.

Sebastian de Calvadores! What was he doing here, and who was he with?

Her face paled as he stared contemptuously at her, suddenly acutely aware of her thin silk nightgown and tousled hair, Colin's hand on her arm, his lips brushing her cheek. Her face flamed as she realised what interpretation Sebastian de Calvadores would be placing on their intimacy, and then berated herself for her embarrassment. Why should she care if he thought she and Colin were lovers? What possible business was it of his? And yet his steely glance seemed to say that he knew everything there was to know about her, and that he doubted that her motives for being with Colin were any less altruistic than those he had accredited her with in his brother's case.

'Jess, is something wrong?' Colin asked her with a frown, sensing her lack of attention. 'You've seemed strangely on edge ever since I arrived. It's that damned cousin of yours, I suppose.'

'Nothing's wrong, I'm just a little tired,' she lied huskily, glad when Sebastian and his companion turned the corner of the corridor. 'I'll be fine in the morning.'

CHAPTER THREE

As a prediction it wasn't entirely true; Jessica felt strangely on edge and tense, her muscles clenching every time someone walked into the dining-room where they were having breakfast.

She would be glad to get back home, she thought wryly as her nerves jumped for the third time in succession at the sight of a dark-haired man. Arrogant brute! He hadn't even given her an opportunity to explain, denouncing her as though she were some female predator and his brother her completely innocent victim. She thought about what she had learned from Isabel and grimaced slightly. How could her cousin have behaved in such an unprincipled way? She had always had a streak of wildness, a tendency to ignore any attempts to curb her headstrong nature, but to actually try and force Jorge into marriage . . . And that was what she had done, no matter how one tried to wrap up the truth, Jessica admitted unhappily. Even so, that was no reason for Sebastian de Calvadores to speak to *her* in the way he had.

'Time to leave for the exhibition,' Colin reminded her, dragging her mind back to the real purpose of her visit to Seville.

Half an hour later they were there, both of them lost in admiration of the fabrics on display.

'Just feel this suede,' Colin murmured to her.

'It's as supple as silk. It makes my fingers itch to use it!'

'And these tweeds!' Jessica exclaimed. 'The wool comes from South America, I believe?'

'Many Spaniards have family connections in South America,' Colin reminded her, 'and I suppose it's only natural that they should turn those connections to commercial advantage, in this case by importing the wool in its raw state, and dying and weaving it here in Spain.'

He drew Jessica's attention to the display belonging to the company they were to see. 'In a class of its own, isn't it?' he asked, watching the way she handled the supple fabric. 'And those colours!'

'They're incredibly subtle,' Jessica agreed with a touch of envy.

On leaving college her first intention had been to find a job in a design capacity with one of the large manufacturers, but such jobs were hard to come by—even harder with the downturn in the textile industry in Britain, and although her languages had stood her in good stead, she had found that without exception the Continental firms preferred to take on their own young graduates. Now working with cloth in its raw stages was only a pipe-dream.

There was quite a busy throng around the Calvortex display and it was several minutes before Colin could talk to one of the young men in charge. He explained his purpose in Seville, producing the letters of recommendation he had brought with him, while Jessica swiftly translated.

'Unfortunately I am merely a member of the staff,' the young man exclaimed regretfully to

Jessica, 'but I will certainly mention this matter to my superiors. If we have a telephone number where we can reach you?'

Handing him both his card and their telephone number at the hotel, Colin announced that they had done enough for one morning and that it was time for lunch. Typically he decided that they would lunch, not at the restaurant within the exhibition, but at another one, far more expensive and exclusive, as Jessica could tell at a glance when their taxi stopped outside it.

She was wearing another of his outfits, and attracted several admiring looks from the other diners as they were shown to their table, Colin beaming delightedly at the attention they were receiving.

Over lunch though he was more serious. 'I hope I do manage to get to some arrangement with Calvortex,' he confided.

Jessica, sensitive to his mood, picked up the tone of worry in his voice.

'It would be very pleasant,' she agreed, 'their fabrics are fantastic, but it won't be the end of the world if we don't, will it?'

'It could be,' Colin told her gravely. 'Things haven't been going too well this last couple of years. The people with money to spend on haute couture are getting fewer and fewer, and we don't exactly produce high fashion stuff. Calvortex fabrics have a world-wide reputation, if we could use them for our clothes I'm convinced it would help boost sales—I've already had one approach from the Americans, with the proviso that we use Calvortex. Somehow they got to hear that we hoped to do so, and they've suggested an excellent contract. There'd be enough profit in it for us to start a cheaper line—bread and butter money coming in with the designer collections as the icing.'

What he said made sense, and Jessica knew enough about the fashion world to know he wasn't exaggerating. Several of the larger fashion houses were cutting back; designers came, were acclaimed for a couple of seasons, and then simply disappeared, but it was like chilly fingers playing down her spine to realise that Colin might be in financial difficulties.

'Well,' Colin told her when they had finished eating, 'let's get back to the exhibition and see if we can find something to fall back on if we don't get anywhere with Calvortex, although I'm afraid if we don't we'll lose the American contract—and one can see why. The texture and colour of those tweeds they were showing . . .'

'Mmm,' Jessica agreed, 'they were marvellous. I wonder how they manage to get such subtle colours?'

'I don't know. I've heard it's a closely guarded secret. Their Chairman is also their main designer and colour expert. It's quite a small concern really, but as I said before, extremely exclusive.'

The rest of the exhibition, while interesting, fell very far short of the standard of the Calvortex display, although Jessica did think that some of the supple leathers and suedes might prove useful to them. For some time she had been trying to persuade Colin to try a younger, more fashionable line, and she could just see those suedes, in pewters, steel-blues and soft greens, in flaring culottes and swirling skirts, topped with chunky hand-knits.

It was shortly after dinner that Colin received a message from reception to say that there had been a call from from Calvortex.

'Stage one completed successfully at least!' he announced to Jessica when he returned to the bar, faintly flushed and obviously excited. 'I've spoken to the Chairman and he's agreed to see me tomorrow. I've explained to him that I've got my assistant with me, so he's arranged for us to tour the factory, and afterwards we can talk.'

She wouldn't be included in the talks, of course, Jessica reflected, but it wouldn't be too difficult a task to occupy herself for a couple of hours—in fact she would enjoy seeing how such beautiful fabrics were made.

Although Colin had not suggested that she did so, she dressed with particular care for the visit— an outfit chosen from their new season's designs, a cream silk blouse and a russet velvet suit with a tiny boxy jacket with narrow puffed sleeves and scrolls of self-coloured embroidery down the front. The skirt fell smoothly in soft loose pleats from the narrow waistband, and it was an outfit that Jessica knew suited her.

Colin obviously thought so too, because he beamed with approval when he saw her.

'Very apt,' he approved as he looked at her. 'The jacket has a certain matador air, very much suited to this part of the world, and I must say I'm very pleased with the way that embroidery has worked out. The colour suits you as well.'

'I thought about the tweed,' Jessica told him, referring to a tweed suit which was also part of the new collection, 'but as it doesn't compare favourably with their fabrics, I thought . . .'

'Quite right,' he approved. 'Now, I've ordered a taxi for us, we've just about got time for a cup of coffee before it arrives.'

He looked more like an Old Etonian than a famous designer, Jessica reflected, eyeing his sober Savile Row suit and immaculate silk shirt. Colin belonged to an older generation that believed in dressing correctly and that one could always tell a gentleman by his clothes; in Colin's case expensive and discreet clothes—Turnbull & Asser shirts and handmade shoes.

The factory was situated just outside Seville, surprisingly modern and with access to the river and the port. It was, as Colin pointed out, very well planned, close to main roads and other facilities, and when he gave in their names at the gates they swung open to allow their vehicle to enter.

They were met in the foyer by a smiling dark-haired young man, dressed formally in a dark suit, his glance for them both extremely respect-ful, although there was a gleam of male interest in the dark eyes as they discreetly examined Jessica.

Having introduced himself as Ramón Ferres, he told them that he was to escort them round the factory.

'Unfortunately the Conde cannot show you round himself,' he explained in the sibilant, liquid English of the Spaniard, 'but he will be free to have lunch with you as arranged,' he informed Colin. 'Forgive me if I stare,' he added to Jessica, 'but we did not realise when Señor Weaver mentioned an assistant that he was talking of a woman. I'm afraid you might find the chemical processes of the factory a little boring . . .'

'Never,' Colin interrupted with a chuckle, while Jessica suppressed a tiny flare of anger at their escort's chauvinistic remark. Of course in Spain things were different. On the whole women were content to take a back seat to live their own lives, especially in the more wealthy families. No doubt someone such as Sebastian de Calvadores' wife, if indeed he had one, would never dream of interfering in her husband's life, or of questioning him about it. That was how they were brought up; to be docile and biddable, content with their families and their homes.

'You'll find that Jessica is far more knowledgeable about the manufacturing process than I am,' Colin added to their guide. 'In fact I suspect she prefers designing fabrics to designing clothes, if the truth were known.'

'Both fascinate me,' Jessica said truthfully.

The next couple of hours flew past. There was so much to see, so much to learn. The factory was the most up-to-date she had ever seen, the equipment of such a sophisticated and superior type that she could only marvel at the technological advances made since she had left college.

They were shown the dying vats, but prudently Ramón Ferres said nothing about how they managed to produce their delicate, subtle colours. All he would say in answer to Jessica's questions was that in the main they used natural and vegetable dyes.

'But surely there's always a problem in stabilising such colours?' she pressed him.

He smiled and shrugged slim shoulders. 'This is so,' he agreed, 'but we have been lucky enough to discover a way of stabilising them—I cannot tell you how, you understand, but be assured that we have done so.'

'And next season's range?' Jessica queried. 'Could we . . .'

Again Ramón Ferres shook his head. 'That is for the Conde to decide,' he explained. He glanced at his watch. 'I will escort you back to the foyer, it is almost time for lunch.' He glanced at Jessica. 'Originally it was intended that we should lunch together, but as I explained, we had expected Señor Weaver's assistant to be a man.'

It was plain that he had expected Colin's assistant to want to talk shop over lunch, and it exasperated Jessica that he should think that simply because she was a woman she was merely paying lip-service to appearing interested.

'I should love to have lunch with you,' she said firmly. 'There are several points I should like to clarify regarding the manufacturing processes; problems you might have in maintaining the quality of your wool, for instance . . .'

They were back in the foyer, and an elegant, dark-haired secretary came to conduct Colin into the Chairman's private sanctum, leaving Jessica with Ramón Ferres.

A little to her surprise he guided her out to car, explaining that although the factory had a restaurant, they operated a scheme similar to that adopted by the Japanese, in that all the staff dined together.

'While the food is excellent, the atmosphere is no conductive to a serious discussion. However, there is a restaurant not far from here.'

'And the Chairman?' Jessica asked curiously, visions of Colin in his Savile Row suit sitting down to eat with several hundred noisy Spaniards.

'He has a private dining room in his suite which he uses for business entertaining.'

As Ramón Ferres had said, the restaurant was not very far away. It had once been the shipping office of a wine exporter, he explained when Jessica expressed interest, but had now been converted into a restaurant.

As they walked inside the unusual barrel-vaulted ceiling caught Jessica's attention, and as they were shown to their table Ramón told her that there were deep cellars beneath the ground.

'Almost every house in Seville has its cellars—a legacy from the times of the Moors—places of sanctuary and safety.'

'And sometimes prisons,' said Jessica, shivering a little. Like most people she found something distinctly frightening about the thought of being imprisoned underground.

'That too,' he agreed. 'The thought distresses you? There are not many of our leading families in Seville who have not had recourse to their cellars, for one reason or another, at some time in their history.'

'This is a very fascinating part of Spain,' Jessica commented as they were served with chilled *gazpacho*. 'A true mingling of East and West.'

'Not always with happy results,' Ramón told her. 'The Moorish character is a proud one, sombre too, and those in Seville who can trace their line back to the Moors are inordinately proud of their bloodlines. It has not always been so, of course. There was a time, during the Inquisition in particular, when to own to Moorish blood was to sign one's own death warrant.'

'Do you have Moorish ancestors?' Jessica asked him, genuinely interested.

He shook his head ruefully. 'No, my family was originally from the north, but the Conde can trace his family back to a knight attached to the Court of Pedro the Cruel. It is said that he ravished away the daughter of his arch-enemy, although there is a legend in the Conde's family that this was not so; that the girl was seduced by her cousin and in fear of her father she laid the blame at the door of his most bitter enemy. The Conde's ancestor was a proud man, and rather than endure the slur on his good name he offered to marry the girl—that is the story passed down through the Conde's family.'

And it bore a sombre echo of truth, Jessica thought wryly. She could well imagine a man who could not be moved by any other emotion being moved by pride; pride in his name and his race. She could almost see the dark flash of bitter eyes as he was faced with his crime . . . She shook herself mentally; what was the matter with her? For a moment in her mind's eye she had mentally imagined Sebastian de Calvadores as that accused ravisher. She would really have to stop thinking about the man. What was the matter with her? She was behaving like a teenager! If she felt anything for him it could only be contempt—and yet when he had stood there saying those dreadful things to her she had longed to tell him the truth, to see him smile instead of frown.

It was Jessica's turn to frown now. Why should she care whether Sebastian de Calvadores frowned or smiled? It was immaterial to her; not that she was ever likely to see him again anyway!

Ramón Ferres was an entertaining companion, and although Jessica suspected that he did not entirely approve of a woman in what he plainly considered to be a man's world, he answered all her questions as pleasantly and fully as he could.

'Much of this you will have to ask the Conde,' he told her with another of his shrugs, when she had asked several highly technical questions. 'I'm afraid I am employed more as a public relations manager than a technical expert. The Conde, on the other hand, knows everything there is to know about the manufacturing process. The whole thing was his brain-child; he conceived the idea when he was in South America working on the *rancho* of his godfather—it is from there that he gets the wool; it is of the highest quality and the partnership is a good one. It is said that Señor Cusuivas would like it to be even closer— he has a daughter who would make the Conde an excellent wife. Forgive me,' he added hastily, 'I should not have said that. The Conde . . .'

'I've forgotten it already,' Jessica assured him, amused that he had so far forgotten himself to gossip a little with her. As he had said himself, he was not from Southern Spain, and perhaps a little homesick here among the more taciturn, secretive people of Seville, who had lived too long in the shadow of death and danger not to weigh their words carefully. Centuries of blood- shed had stained this soil, leaving the inhabitants

a legacy of caution—deep-seated and ineradic-
able.

'I shall have to leave you in the foyer for a few
minutes,' Ramón apologised to her when they got
back to the factory. 'Señor Weaver should not be
long, and I'm afraid I have some business to
attend to, but I shall leave you in Constancia's
capable hands.'

Constancia was the secretary. She gave Jessica
a brief smile, and offered a cup of coffee. Jessica
accepted; the wine with their lunch had left her
feeling thirsty.

The girl had been gone about five minutes
when the door behind her desk was suddenly
thrust open.

'Constancia . . .'

Jessica felt her heart lurch in recognition of the
voice, less grim than when she had heard it last, but
recognisable all the same. She was halfway out of
her seat, the blood draining from her face, when
Sebastian de Calvadores turned and saw her,
frowning in disbelief. '*Dios!*' he swore angrily.
'You would pursue me even here? Have you no
pride, no natural feminine reticence? I have told
you as plainly as I can, *señorita*, that my brother has
no interest in you. And nor will you find him here.
He is away from home at the moment, visiting the
family of his *novia*-to-be,' he added cruelly, 'a
young girl of excellent family who would rather die
than tell a man to whom she was not married that
she was to bear his child.'

This last gibe brought the hot colour back to
Jessica's face.

'Did you send your brother away so that he
couldn't see . . . me?' she asked heatedly.

'Hardly. I had no prior warning of your arrival. However, I am sure that had we done so, Jorge would have thanked me for saving him from an unpleasant confrontation. What did you hope for by coming here? To browbeat him into changing his mind and offering you the protection of his name—our name?' he added proudly.

Before Jessica could retaliate the door opened again and Colin came out, beaming as he caught sight of her.

'Ah, Jessica my dear, you're back. Conde,' he smiled, turning to Sebastian de Calvadores and astounding Jessica, 'allow me to introduce my assistant to you. Jessica—the Conde de Calvadores, Chairman of Calvortex!'

'This is your assistant of whom you have spoken so highly to me?' Just for a moment Jessica saw that Sebastian was practically dumbfounded, although he managed to conceal his shock faster than she could hers.

He was the Chairman of Calvortex! He was the person on whom the future success of Colin's business depended. Her heart sank. She couldn't see him agreeing to anything that involved her, no matter how remotely.

'Yes, this is Jessica,' Colin was agreeing happily, plainly unaware of any undercurrents. 'Like Señor Ferres, the Conde expected my assistant to be a man,' he added to Jessica.

'Perhaps because I'm a woman he would prefer to see me shut away behind a locked gate—or better still, in one of Seville's many dungeons,' Jessica said lightly, and although Colin laughed, she knew from the tiny muscle clenching in the

Conde's lean jaw that he had not missed her point.

'The Conde has invited me to join him for dinner this evening,' Colin told her. 'We have still not discussed everything.'

Jessica's heart pounded. Was the discovery that she was Colin's assistant going to affect his decision adversely? Surely as a businessman Sebastian de Calvadores would make his final judgment on commercial grounds only, and yet she couldn't help remembering what Ramón Ferres had said about his family and how it tied in with her own impression that he was an inordinately proud man. Would he turn Colin's suggestions down simply because Colin employed her?

Constancia returned with her cup of coffee and Jessica took it, grateful for an excuse to turn away from Sebastian de Calvadores' bitter eyes.

What an appalling coincidence! She had never imagined for one moment that Jorge's arrogant brother and the head of Calvortex would be one and the same man.

'. . . and of course, Jessica is of particular help to me because she speaks several languages fluently,' she suddenly heard Colin saying, and her fingers trembled as they curled round the coffee cup and she realised that the two men were discussing her.

'Most fortuitous,' she heard Sebastian de Calvadores replying, cynicism underlining the words, and bringing a faint flush to her pale skin. 'I believe you told me that she was also fully qualified in textile design and processing?'

'Oh yes,' Colin beamed. 'In fact that's really

her first love, but as I'm sure you know, we have nothing in England to rival anything such as Calvortex.'

'I believe you mentioned that you would like to use the telephone,' Jessica heard Sebastian murmuring to Colin. 'If you would care to go with my secretary, she will help you with your calls.'

As Colin followed Constancia into her office, Jessica had a cowardly impulse to beg him not to leave her alone with Sebastian de Calvadores.

'Quite a coincidence,' he observed coldly when they were alone, 'and one that makes me even more suspicious of your motives. You knew, of course, when you first met Jorge of his connection with Calvortex and from that doubtless deduced that he was a comparatively wealthy young man. For all your much vaunted feminism and independence I find you are very little different from our own women in that you are looking for a man who will support you and ease your way through life, although unlike them you do not have the honesty to admit it, nor the accomplishments to make the bait tempting, especially not to a Spaniard, who expects to find his bride pure and innocent. No wonder you went for a boy like Jorge! He is still young enough to find a certain charm in experience—of course it is expected that young men will ... experiment, but you are singularly foolish if you honestly believe that Jorge would marry a woman such as yourself.'

Jessica's hand snaked out—she couldn't help it—anything to destroy that cynical, infuriating smile. But the instant her palm made contact with the lean tanned cheek, a sick wave of self-disgust swept over her. What on earth was happening to her? She had never struck anyone in anger before, no matter how much she had been provoked.

And it seemed that Sebastian de Calvadores shared her shock. His fingers touched the faintly reddening flesh, his eyes darkening rapidly to a fury that scorched and terrified her, but Jessica refused to be cowed. No matter how much she was trembling inwardly, he would never be allowed to know of it!

'*Dios*, vixen!' The words were breathed harshly, fastidious disgust etched in every line of the aristocratic features. 'Nobody strikes a Calvadores and is allowed /to escape without retribution!'

He moved, silent and agile as a cougar, grasping her wrists and pinioning them with hard fingers that locked onto her tender flesh. She tried to pull away, infuriated by her sudden imprisonment, and with a speed that left her startled and breathless she was jerked forward, the fingers that had held her wrists, grasping onto her shoulders, the dark grey eyes smouldering with an anger that touched off something elemental deep within her own body, mutual antagonism crackling between them.

'*Cristos!*'

She heard Sebastian swear and then his mouth was on hers, angry and hatefully contemptuous— the very worst kind of punishment, letting her know that she was less than the dust beneath his feet, her breasts were crushed against the fine wool of his suit and it appalled her that such a

bitter and punishing embrace should still have
the power to ignite a powerful sexual chemistry
so that she was aware of Sebastian de Calvadores
as a man in a way that she could never remember
being aware of any man before. The expensive
suit and silk shirt were simply the trappings of
civilisation masking the true nature of a man who
was still every bit as much a conqueror as his
ancestors had been. He was enjoying using his
body to punish her—she could sense it, feel it in
the hard arrogance of his flesh against hers,
forcing her to submit.

Against her will her lips softened, trembling
slightly beneath the determined assault. Almost
instantly Sebastian drew away.

'I am not my brother, Señorita James,' he told
her sardonically. 'The warmth of your mouth
trembling beneath mine leaves me cold—especially when I know that I am far from being the
first man to have tasted its sweetness.'

'How hypocritical of you!' Jessica flashed back,
walking unsteadily away from him. 'You obviously expect your wife, when you eventually
marry, to be as pure as the driven snow, but you,
I feel sure, can make no such claims!'

'Would you give a Stradivarius violin or a
Bechstein piano to a mere beginner?' he mocked
back, astounding her with his cynicism. 'And I
think you need not concern yourself with the
views of the woman who will be my wife,
Señorita James. You and she will be worlds apart
in your views on life.'

'Just like me and the girl Jorge is to marry,'
Jessica stormed at him, irrationally hurt by his
comment. 'How do I know Jorge really wants to

marry this girl? How do I know it's not simply your idea?'

'Jesu Maria!' Sebastian breathed, as though imploring the heavens for patience. 'Jorge has told you himself!'

'Perhaps because you insisted,' Jessica told him doggedly, not sure why she was needling him like this, except that it had something to do with the contempt in his eyes when he had released her after kissing her. 'Perhaps I should get in touch with Jorge myself, talk to him . . .'

'Never! I will not allow it!'

He looked so grimly implacable that Jessica felt a tiny frisson of fear. Why on earth had she goaded him like that? She knew she had no intention of saying anything to Jorge! And yet something seemed to drive her on, so that she shrugged and said nonchalantly:

'You couldn't stop me.'

She almost flinched when she saw the look of utter fury in his eyes; eyes that had darkened almost to black, only the pale grey rim shimmering with barely suppressed rage as he stared at her.

'You dare to challenge me?' he demanded with awesome control. 'You are not only venal, you are a fool as well!' he told her softly.

CHAPTER FOUR

'YOU'RE quite sure you'll be all right?' Colin asked her fussily for the fourth time.

Jessica sighed. 'You're going out for the evening, not leaving me on the steps of the workhouse,' she reminded him dryly. 'Of course I'll be all right, what on earth could possibly happen to me?'

It was eight-thirty before Colin left for his dinner engagement with Sebastian de Calvadores, and after he had gone Jessica leaned back in her chair in the bar and tried to relax.

Her nerves had been like coiled springs ever since they left the factory. She had alternated between longing to confide in Colin and a firm determination not to involve him in her private affairs.

Sebastian de Calvadores couldn't possibly deprive Colin of the contract simply because he employed her, surely? And yet there had been a look in his eyes just before Colin had rejoined them which suggested that he would be perfectly willing to journey to hell and back again if he thought that by doing so he could punish her.

And what better way of punishing her could there be than putting Colin's business at risk? It wasn't inconceivable if things didn't improve that Colin would be forced to let her go, and she had no delusions about herself. In spite of her qualifications and experience she would find it extremely difficult to get a job of equivalent standing.

Against her will she found herself remembering Sebastian's kiss—in no way meant to be an affectionate embrace, but rather a gesture of disdain and condemnation—her memory lingering on the hard length of his body against hers, disturbingly male.

She went up to her room before Colin returned, mentally crossing her fingers that all would go well. He had been full of optimism when he set out, and she only hoped that it was well founded.

'So how did things go last night?'

Colin looked up from his breakfast, and it seemed to Jessica that he avoided her eyes as he answered, 'Quite well. The Conde seemed very interested in my proposals.'

'Did he agree to them, then?' Jessica pressed, for some reason alarmed by Colin's hesitancy.

'In a manner of speaking, although there were certain conditions . . .'

'Only to be expected in view of his company's reputation,' Jessica agreed, her spirits lightening. 'What were they?'

For a moment Colin didn't speak, and several seconds later when Jessica replaced her coffee cup she found him regarding her with an expression compounded of uncertainty and appeal. Suspicion sharpened her gaze, fear sending the blood pounding through her veins. Sebastian had told him he would only give him the contract if Colin got rid of her!

'He wants you to fire me, doesn't he?' she said calmly. 'Oh, I . . .'

'No, no, Jessica, it's not that,' Colin quickly reassured her. 'Quite the contrary. It seems that they're having problems with the designs for their next collection of fabrics. The Conde works on them himself with the help of another designer, whom he has recently lost to a rival organisation. As you can imagine, the Conde is most anxious to complete the work on the season's designs, and he's asked me if I would be agreeable to you working for him until this is done.'

Whatever Jessica expected to hear it was not this! For a few minutes she was too astounded to say anything.

'You see, you were quite wrong in thinking he disapproved of you,' Colin told her. 'He seemed most impressed when I told him about your qualifications. Over dinner tonight he questioned me in detail about you—where you'd trained, how long you'd worked for me. I must admit that I had no idea what he was leading up to, but it seems that Ramón Ferres had told him how interested you were in the manufacturing processes and how knowledgeable, and he confided to me the difficult situation he finds himself in.'

'But surely a firm such as Calvortex would have no trouble at all in finding a junior designer,' Jessica suggested, feeling a tinge of suspicion. Why did Sebastian want her to work for him? She couldn't understand it, especially when he had let her know how much he despised her and how determined he was to keep her away from his brother.

'Certainly,' Colin agreed, 'but it seems he's reluctant to take someone on on a permanent basis at this stage—employing someone on a temporary basis would suit him admirably, but as he admitted to me, it's very difficult to find an accomplished designer willing to be employed for a mere matter of weeks. It seems the Conde has a brother who may eventually take the place of the departed designer, but he needs a designer now to help him complete the new season's range of fabrics. It's quite an honour that he should ask for you,' he pointed out logically, 'and you've always said how much you'd like to work in textiles. It would only be for a few weeks—I should hold your job for you, of course—we can do nothing on next season's designs in any case until we know what fabrics Calvortex will produce.'

'Is your contract dependent on my agreeing to work for the Conde?' Jessica asked, frowning. She could not understand why the Conde would make such a stipulation, but if he had it could not be for any reason that would benefit her.

'Not in so many words,' Colin told her wryly, 'but I suspect if you did refuse . . .'

He left the sentence unfinished, but Jessica felt she knew enough about the Conde to guess at the pressure he would bring to bear on her employer. Despite her love of textiles she had not the slightest desire to work for Sebastian de Calvadores. But if she refused Colin's company might well fold. What should she do? Not for the first time she found herself wishing there was someone she could turn to for advice, instead of always being the giver of advice to others.

'What's wrong?' Colin asked her hesitantly. 'I thought you'd jump at the chance.'

'It's such a surprise,' Jessica told him, not untruthfully. 'How long would it mean staying in Spain?'

'I'm not sure. The details would have to be arranged with the Conde. Initially he is merely enquiring if I would be prepared to let you go on a temporary basis, and if you would be prepared to work for Calvortex. One other thing . . .' he paused and glanced at her uncertainly. 'He did suggest that he would be prepared to pay you extremely well.'

He would, Jessica thought cynically, her fingers curling into her palms, an irate expression in her eyes, and for one heady moment she toyed with the idea of telling the Conde exactly what he could do with both his job and his money. And then common sense intruded, bringing her back down to earth. Colin was watching her with a heartrendingly pathetic expression, and she knew she simply hadn't the heart to tell him she was going to refuse. It was a golden opportunity, she told herself, trying to cheer herself up; she would undoubtedly learn a considerable amount, and in years to come it would stand her in good stead to say she had worked for Calvortex, no matter how briefly, if she wanted to obtain another job.

'You'll do it?' Colin said eagerly, correctly interpreting her expression.

'I don't see that I've got much option,' she agreed dryly.

'Good! I'll telephone the Conde and give him the good news. Doubtless he'll want to talk to you to finalise all the arrangements.'

'Doubtless,' Jessica echoed ironically. She

could well imagine the sneering expression and suffocating arrogance Sebastian would adopt when he knew that she had agreed to his suggestion.

A tiny seed of doubt had taken root in her subconscious, warning her that she would regret this weakness, but she couldn't see what Sebastian could possibly do to her other than attempt to make her life a misery with his cynical remarks and contemptuous eyes, and she would soon show him that she was completely impervious to both.

Jessica had just stepped into the shower when she heard someone knocking on her door. Thinking it must be the maid with the light meal she had ordered, she shrugged on her towelling robe and quickly opened the door.

To her consternation it was not a maid who stood there, but Sebastian de Calvadores, looking cynically urbane as he lounged carelessly against the open door, his eyes slowly appraising her.

'I thought you were room service,' she stammered, feeling as gauche as a raw teenager. 'I . . . what did you want?'

'To speak to you. Surely Colin has already apprised you of my suggestion?'

'You want to speak about that? But Colin said you were going to telephone . . . at least . . .' She couldn't remember now exactly what Colin *had* said; Sebastian's unexpected appearance had thrown her completely, her thoughts were a chaotic muddle.

'Are you going to invite me in, or shall we hold our discussion here in full view of the other guests? On balance I think we would be better inside,' he drawled, walking past her and calmly closing the door.

'But I'm not dressed . . .' Jessica protested, hot colour storming her face as he looked her over thoughtfully.

'An age-old ploy, but one that unfortunately does not work on me. I'm immune to women who use their bodies as you use yours.'

'And yet you still want me to work for you? I should have thought I would be the last person you would want in your employ.'

'Sometimes it is necessary to give way to expediency,' he told her crisply. 'Now, could I trouble you for your decision?'

He really was the most unbearably arrogant man she had ever met in her life! Jessica thought wrathfully. Anyone with the slightest pretensions to consideration would have suggested that they meet downstairs, or at least have given her an opportunity to dress, but not Sebastian de Calvadores. No doubt he enjoyed having her at a disadvantage!

'I can't believe you want me to work for you,' she protested, wishing he would not watch her so closely. She felt like a particularly obnoxious life form being viewed beneath a microscope.

'Come, I'm sure I do not need to boost your ego by paying you flattering compliments. I am assured by your employer that you are a first-class designer. He is a man whose judgment I trust—I need a designer badly enough to be prepared to overlook certain aspects of your personality. It is as simple as that.'

'You must want me very badly if you were

prepared to threaten Colin that you would withdraw the contract!'

'As I said before, it is a matter of expediency. I am already behind with work on next season's fabrics. There have been problems with some of the dyes. Primarily I am a chemist, not a designer, and the work I have had to do on this side of things has meant that there have been delays in the design end of things. Like any other manufacturer, I have deadlines to meet. My suggestion to Colin was based purely on commercial necessity. He understands this even if you don't. I am prepared to help him if he will help me, there is nothing out of the ordinary in that.'

Nothing at all, and yet still Jessica felt uneasy, as though there was something she wasn't being told; something hidden from her.

'And you will merely want me to work for you for a matter of a few weeks?' she pressed.

'Two months at the most. Señor Weaver has said he can spare you for this length of time—the rest is up to you.' He gave a comprehensive shrug. 'I doubt that I would ever be your choice of employer—Señor Weaver obviously has no idea of your true personality—but if you wish to save his business I am sure you will see the wisdom of agreeing.'

He must want a designer very badly, was Jessica's first thought, but then he had already admitted that he did. So why did she have this nagging feeling that there was something else?

'You . . .' she began.

'I have no time to waste in answering further arguments,' he interrupted her with an arrogance that had her spine prickling as defensively as a ruffled kitten's. 'Either you agree or you refuse, but if you refuse, be very sure at what cost.'

It really wasn't fair, Jessica thought, shivering a little, as she hugged her robe even more firmly around her slender body. What choice did she have?

'I . . . I agree,' she said huskily at last, the tiny thread of disquiet she had felt earlier exploding into full-blown fear as she saw the triumph glittering briefly in his eyes.

'Most wise. So . . . if you will be ready to leave in the morning, I shall collect you at nine, that will leave us enough time to . . .'

'Leave?'

'Ah yes, didn't I tell you?' he drawled mockingly. 'I intend to spend the next two months working from my *hacienda*. I have . . . responsibilities there, and the peace and quiet of the *hacienda* is more conducive to design work than the factory. Besides, it is there that I have my laboratories where we experiment with the dyes.'

'I'm not going with you.'

'Oh, but I think you are,' came the silky response. 'Only five minutes ago you told me that you were prepared to work for me. Surely the mere fact that you have learned that you are to be a guest in my family home instead of living alone in a hotel cannot be the reason for this sudden turn-around. Think of Colin,' he told her hardily, 'think of your own future, just as I am thinking of my brother's.'

'Jorge?' Jessica looked bewildered. 'What does he have to do with this?'

'Everything,' he told her succinctly. 'Did you honestly think I would allow you to remain in Seville to further harass my poor brother upon his return, spreading the lord only knows what rumours about his relationship with you—rumours which could well reach the ears of his *novia*? Seville is a very enclosed society and a very rigid one. Barbara's father would never consider Jorge as a husband for his daughter if he were to learn of his relationship with you.'

'I should have thought it was Barbara's opinion that mattered, not her father's,' Jessica remarked sardonically, watching him look down the aquiline length of his nose at her, 'and besides, I had no intention of staying in Spain.'

'You tell me that now, but you cannot deny you came here initially with the express purpose of seeing my brother, when he had already written to you telling you that your association was at an end? No, even if you swore to me that you would never try to contact Jorge again I would not believe you. There is only one way to end your interference in our lives.'

'And what may that be?' Jessica asked tartly. 'Or does the mere fact that I'm in your employ mean that no one would ever believe a Calvadores guilty of demeaning himself by becoming involved with a mere wage-slave?'

Her sarcasm brought a dark tinge of angry colour seeping beneath his tan, his eyes as cold as granite as he stared at her aloofly.

'By no means,' he said at last, 'but what they will think is that Jorge would never stoop to become involved with my mistress.'

'Your . . . You mean you'd let people think I

was your mistress?' Jessica gasped. 'Oh, this is infamous! You wouldn't dare!'

A muscle clenched in his jaw, beating angrily against the taut skin, and her eyes were drawn betrayingly to it, as it echoed the uneven pounding of her own heart.

'I thought you might have learned by now not to challenge me,' he told her softly, and she knew that he did dare—anything—if he deemed it necessary.

Heavens, it was like a Restoration comedy! First of all he accused her of being his brother's mistress and now he was saying everyone would think she was his!

'You're exaggerating,' she said positively. 'No one would believe, because I was working for you, that I was your mistress.'

'Of course not,' he agreed smoothly, 'if we were working at the factory. But we shall be working at my home, and I shall take good care to make sure that our relationship is not merely that of employer and employee.'

'But this is all so unnecessary!' Jessica cried heatedly.

'To you perhaps, but not to me. The Calvadores name means a great deal to me, and I will not have it dragged in the mud because some greedy woman tries to blackmail my brother into marrying her.'

His last unforgivable words infuriated her. By what right did he presume to stand in judgment on her?

'Well, if you expect to stop me by dragging me off to your *hacienda*, you're in for a big disappointment,' she told him coldly, 'because

I'm not coming with you, and there's no way short of using physical force that you can make me.'

'You've already agreed to work for me,' he pointed out icily, '—of your own free will. If you don't . . .'

'I know,' Jessica agreed wearily. 'Colin will lose the contract.'

'No doubt he will understand—when you explain to him your reasons for refusing,' he told her smoothly, and a sick dismay filled her. Of course she could not explain to Colin why she had refused, it was all far too complicated now, and he would probably simply tell her to tell the truth. How could she do that now? How could she expose Isabel to his wrath? For one thing, she would not put it past him to go to England and terrorise Isabel into doing something foolish. And what about John? How would he react to the news that his fiancée had been having a brief fling in Spain when she was supposed to be thinking over his proposal, and moreover that she had actually thought that she might be pregnant by her lover? No, she could not tell the truth, and the only alternatives were to either accept the proposition and everything that went with it, or refuse it and risk jeopardising Colin's business. Some alternative!

She knew she really had no choice, but it infuriated her to have to give in to such outrageously buccaneering tactics.

'I will come with you,' she said coolly at last, 'but if you attempt to give anyone the impression that we're anything other than business colleagues, I shall be forced to contradict you.'

'Who said anything about "telling" anyone?'
he mocked her softly. 'There are other, more
subtle ways—like this, for instance.'

Before she could stop him, he had jerked her
against his body, his hands locking behind her,
holding her against him. She could feel the steady
thud of his heart, so much at variance with her own
which was racing unsteadily, the breath constricted
in her throat, her eyes on a level with the plain
severity of his tie. Her heightened senses relayed to
her the sharp, clean fragrance of his cologne, the
pristine freshness of his shirt, and the smooth
brown column of his throat. She lifted her eyes.
There was a dark shadow along his jaw suggesting
that he might find it necessary to shave night and
morning, and she shivered at the thoughts the
knowledge conjured up in her mind.

'Let me go!' Her voice was husky, edged with
anger and pain. She saw the curling mockery of
his smile, the darkness of the cold grey eyes, and
knew there was about as much chance of her plea
being answered as there was of a hawk dropping
its prey.

'You are trembling.'

It was a statement that held an edge of
surprise, accompanied by a quick frown. The
hand that wasn't securing her body against the
hard length of his moved to her shoulder, flicking
aside the collar of her robe to reveal the silky
paleness of her skin.

'You didn't do much sunbathing when you
were on holiday, or is it simply that Jorge told
you how much we Latin races admire a palely
beautiful skin? Yours has the translucency of a
pearl.'

His fingers stroked lightly across her exposed collarbone, tiny tendrils of fear curling insidiously through her lower stomach. Oh no, she thought achingly, what was he trying to do to her? What *was* he doing to her? She had been touched before, for heaven's sake—but never with such explicit sensuality; never as though the male fingers drifting against her skin were touching the softest silk.

'*Dios*,' she heard him murmur smokily, 'one would think you had never been touched by a man before. But we both know that is not true, don't we, *señorita*?'

And then, shockingly, his mouth was where his fingers had been, the eroticism of his touch sending tiny shivers of pleasure coursing through her body. Mindlessly Jessica allowed him to mould her body to his, her head falling back helplessly against his arm, his eyes darkening to obsidian as the neckline of her robe dipped, revealing the pale curves of her breasts.

'Like marble,' he murmured huskily, trailing his fingers seductively along the hollow between her breasts, ignoring her stifled gasp of shock, 'but unlike marble, your skin feels warm to my touch.' His fingers tightened ruthlessly on her hair, his voice hardening as he demanded savagely, 'Tell me now that someone walking in here would not immediately think that we were lovers!'

She shivered bitterly with reaction, hating herself for the way she had yielded so completely to his superior strength, hating her body's purely female response to his masculinity.

His sardonic, 'Perhaps you need further

convincing,' made her stomach muscles coil tensely, her body stiffening as he grasped her chin, tilting it so that there was no way she could avoid the hard punishment of his lips, and yet even knowing that he was punishing her, something elemental and fierce sprang to life inside her the moment his mouth touched hers. Her robe was pushed aside, tanned fingers cupping the soft swell of one breast. Jessica shuddered uncontrollably and pushed frantically away, and by some miracle Sebastian released her, surveying her flushed cheeks and furious eyes with cynical amusement.

'What is wrong?' he drawled. 'Surely I took no liberties that have not been permitted to countless others?'

The truth of the matter was that he had; but Jessica wasn't going to admit as much.

'As you've pointed out,' she responded icily, '*they* were permitted them, you weren't.' Not even for Colin's sake could she agree to work with him now; she would never know a moment's peace, never be able to relax . . .

'I'm not going to work for you,' she told him quickly, huddling into the protection of her robe, and avoiding his eyes. 'I . . .'

'You are trying to tell me you won't work for me because of that?' He was openly incredulous and disbelieving. 'You are behaving like an affronted virgin; quite unnecessary, you cannot imagine you stand in any danger of receiving unwanted advances from me? If I haven't already made it clear, perhaps it's time I did,' he told her with deadly silky venom. 'I am not interested in other men's leavings—whether it is

one man or a hundred. You are as safe with me
as you would be locked up in a convent. Don't
mistake a timely warning for any desire for you,
and that was all that was—a warning. You will
come with me,' he added softly, 'I promise you
that. Be ready—I shall pick you up tomorrow
morning at nine.'

If she had any pride, she would be on a plane
back home right now, not sitting staring at her
suitcases and wondering if she was doing the
right thing, Jessica decided as she glanced round
the impersonal hotel bedroom. A glance at her
watch showed that it was half past eight. Colin
had already left for the airport, full of praise and
gratitude—they had talked all evening, and she
had tried on several occasions to tell him that
there was simply no way she could work for
Sebastian de Calvadores, but every time her
nerve failed her.

A knock on her door startled her. The porter
entered and picked up her cases. Nervous dread
fluttering through her stomach, Jessica followed
him to the lift.

To try and calm herself a little she ordered
herself a cup of coffee, but when it came she felt
totally unable to drink it. She hadn't had any
breakfast either. Why, oh, why hadn't she left
Spain with Colin? He would have understood if
she had explained. But she hadn't been able to
disappoint him, to know that she was destroying
everything he had come to Spain to achieve. She
was a coward, she berated herself. She should
have told him, and if she had, she wouldn't be
here now, waiting ... her heart leapt into her

throat as she saw the familiar tall figure striding towards her.

'Come!'

It was the first time she had seen him wearing anything other than a formal suit; the dark, narrow-fitting pants clinging to the taut muscles of his thighs, the thin silk shirt hinting at the shadow of hair across his chest. Her stomach muscles tensed protestingly, and she was vividly reminded of how she had felt when he touched her. A fine linen jacket emphasised the breadth of his shoulders, and Jessica suddenly felt acutely nervous. What did she know of this man, apart from the fact that he had an almost obsessive pride in the good name of his family? Nothing!

'You may cease looking at me as though I had suddenly grown two heads. I assure you, you are quite safe,' he told her urbanely. 'Just as long as you behave yourself.'

'And if I don't, you'll do what?' Jessica demanded huskily. 'Punish me as you did yesterday, by forcing yourself on me?'

'Be careful, Señorita James,' he warned her softly. 'You challenge me so recklessly that I wonder if you find the "punishment" as unpalatable as you claim. You have a saying, do you not, "Any port in a storm", but I will not be the port for your frustrated desires, no matter how much you goad me.'

Jessica stared at him fulminatingly. Did he dare to suggest that she actually wanted him to touch her? To . . .

'You're quite wrong,' she told him bitterly. 'I would rather endure the worst tempest that can rage than seek a haven in your arms!'

Just for a moment she thought she had disconcerted him. There was a brief flash of surprise in his eyes, but then it was gone, and he was ushering her through the foyer to the main entrance of the hotel. Outside, he guided her towards a gleaming Mercedes, while a porter brought out her luggage.

Jessica glanced at the car and shivered slightly. Once she was inside it there would be no going back, no chance to change her mind. She hesitated, torn between a longing to escape no matter what the cost, and a feeling that she owed it to Colin to stay.

'Do not do it,' a dulcet voice murmured in her ear. 'Where would you run to? Come,' Sebastian added, 'get in the car, and stop regarding me as though I were a convicted felon. I assure you I am quite harmless when I am treated with respect.'

Blindly Jessica groped for the rear door handle, but to her surprise, he opened the front passenger door.

'What's the matter?' she asked him bitterly as she climbed in. 'Surely you aren't afraid I'll try and escape?'

'We are supposed to be lovers,' he told her succinctly. 'That being the case, you would not sit alone in the rear of the car.'

'Certainly not,' Jessica agreed sarcastically. 'That, from what I recall of Spanish life, is a privilege accorded only to wives!'

They drove for several kilometres in silence, Jessica's nerves tensing every time Sebastian glanced at her. He was a fast but careful driver. sSe looked surreptitiously at him, flushing when she discovered that he was watching her.

'I have already told you,' he said harshly, 'you have nothing of a sexual nature to fear from me.'

'I don't,' Jessica told him, surprised by the anger in his eyes and the rigid line of his mouth.

'No? You are clutching the edge of your seat as though you expect an imminent assault on your virtue. Or are you simply trying for an effect? If so, it won't work,' he told her laconically. 'Even if I did not know all about you from Jorge, I could never believe that a Northern European woman in her twenties had retained the virginal innocence you are trying to portray.'

'Why not?' Jessica snapped at him. 'That comment has about as much basis for truth as saying that all Spanish girls are virgins when they marry—it simply doesn't hold water.'

'I shall not argue about it,' she was told evenly, 'but if I were you I would not tax my patience too greatly by trying to assimilate a personality we both know you do not possess!'

Jessica didn't know how long it would take them to reach the *hacienda*, but when eleven o'clock came and went and they were in the depths of the country she started to realise how difficult it might be for her to leave the *hacienda* if she wished.

'Not much farther now,' Sebastian told her. 'Another hour, perhaps.'

'How on earth can you work so far away from the factory?' Jessica asked him.

'There are such things as telephones,' he told her dryly. 'The *hacienda* has been in my family for many generations. We still grow the grapes that go to make one of our fine local sherries, although now this is not produced exclusively from Calvadores vines.'

Jessica had already noticed the vines growing in the fields, but pride had prevented her from asking too many questions—that and a growing nausea exacerbated by the fact that she had had no breakfast. In fact she was beginning to feel distinctly lightheaded, but she forced herself to appear alert and interested as Sebastian told her about the local wines, and the art of making sherry.

It was almost exactly twelve o'clock when they turned off the main road, throwing up clouds of dust as they bumped down an unmade-up track. Vines covered the ground as far as the eye could see, and it was only when they crested a small incline that Jessica got her first glimpse of the hacienda.

For some reason she had expected a simple farmhouse-type building, and she caught her breath in awe as she stared down at the collection of Moorish-style buildings, shimmering whitely in the strong sunlight, the cupolas gilded by the sun, for all the world as though the entire complex had been wafted from ancient Baghdad on a magic carpet.

'The original building was constructed many centuries ago by an ancestor of mine,' Sebastian told her. 'He was given this land as part of his wife's dowry and on it he built the first house. Since then many generations have added to it, but always retaining the Moorish flavour—of course there have been times, for instance during the Inquisition, when it was not always wise for people to admit to their Moorish blood, when it has even perhaps been expedient to deny it.'

Looking at him, Jessica couldn't imagine that he would ever deny his heritage; indeed, she could far more easily see him condemning himself to the flames of the *auto de Fe* than recanting his Moorish blood and his proud ancestors.

They drove under a white archway and into an outer courtyard, paved and cool. As Sebastian opened her door for her, Jessica was aware of movements, of a door opening and people hurrying towards them. A wave of dizziness struck her, and she clung hard to the nearest solid object, distracted to realise it was Sebastian's arm, and then, catching her completely off guard, Sebastian bent his head, coolly capturing her lips and plundering the unguarded sweetness of her mouth.

Just for a moment time seemed to stand still, crazily improbable emotions racing through her heart. What was happening to her that she should want to cling to those broad shoulders and go on clinging? And then her lips were released and Sebastian was saying lazily, in English, 'Ah, Tia Sofia, allow me to introduce Jessica.'

And Jessica was being scrutinised thoughtfully by a pair of snapping dark eyes, very much like Sebastian's, although in a feminine and less arrogant face.

'You are on time, Sebastian,' was all his aunt said. 'The little one is so excited I have had to tell her to go and lie down for a little while. It is always the same when she knows you are coming.'

'My aunt refers to my ... ward,' Sebastian explained to Jessica. 'She lives here at the *hacienda* with my aunt and will do so until she is old enough to go to school.' His fingers rested lightly on her arm, and although she was looking discreetly away, Jessica knew that his aunt was aware of their intimacy.

'I have had Rosalinda's rooms prepared for your guest,' she was saying to Sebastian, glancing uncertainly at him.

'Rosalinda was the first Calvadores bride to occupy the *hacienda*,' Sebastian told Jessica. 'Her rooms are in one of the towers, quite secluded from the rest of the house with their own courtyard and stairs leading from it.'

Jessica's face flamed as the implication of his words sank in, and out of the corner of her eye she saw his aunt frown a little and glance at her uncertainly. There was no doubt at all in Jessica's mind that his aunt thought that they were lovers. Lovers! A sharp pain seemed to stab through her heart, her muscles tensing in protest at the images the word invoked. But she and Sebastian were not lovers, she reminded herself, nor ever likely to be. For one thing, he felt nothing but contempt for her, while she, of course, equally detested him ... Just for a moment she remembered her mixed emotions when he had kissed her, quickly banishing the treacherous suggestion that there had been something infinitely pleasurable in the pressure of his mouth against hers. How could it have been remotely pleasurable? He had kissed her in punishment and she had loathed and resented it! Of course she had.

CHAPTER FIVE

IT was Sebastian's aunt who showed Jessica to Rosalinda's tower, much to her relief.

They approached the tower via a narrow, spiralling staircase, the smoothly plastered walls decorated with decorative frescoes and friezes in the Arabic style.

At the top of the stairs, Tia Sofia opened a door and gestured to Jessica to precede her. Once inside Jessica caught her breath on a gasp of pleasure. The room was large and octagonal in shape, an arched doorway leading to another room, and the view from the mediaeval slit windows stunned her with the magnificent panorama spread out below.

'This room is the highest in the house,' Sofia de Calvadores explained. 'Although latterly it has not been used—it is too impractical for a married couple, and there have been no daughters of the house to make it their own as was the custom in the past.'

'It's beautiful,' Jessica said reverently, gazing at her surroundings. The walls were hung with a soft apricot silk, matching rugs on the polished wood floor. This room was furnished as a small sitting room, and she guessed that beyond it lay the bedroom. Bookcases had been built to fit the octagonal walls; one of the larger window embrasures was fitted with a cushioned seat, and it wasn't hard to imagine a lovely Spanish girl sitting there perhaps playing her mandolin while she gazed through the window waiting for her husband to return home.

Her guide opened the communicating door to show Jessica the bedroom, once again decorated in the same soft apricot, the huge bed covered with a soft silk coverlet.

'There is a bathroom through there,' she told Jessica, indicating another door set into one of the walls. 'It is fortunate that when the idea of this octagonal room was conceived it was built within the existing square tower, so we have been able to make use of the space between the walls to install modern plumbing. I shall leave you now—Maria will come and unpack for you, and we normally have lunch at one.'

Taking the gentle hint, as soon as she was alone Jessica opened the bathroom door, gasping with fresh delight when she saw the sunken marble bath and mirrored walls of the room, reflecting images of her whichever way she turned, the mirrors possessing a greenish tinge, given off by the malachite.

She washed quickly, then changed into a linen skirt in a buttercup yellow shade that complemented her colouring, adding a delicate short-sleeved embroidered blouse. She was going to need more clothes if she was to stay here for the time stipulated. She would have to write to her aunt and ask her to arrange to send some of her things on.

She checked her make-up, renewing her lipstick, chagrined to see how little of it was left after Sebastian's kiss, and having brushed her hair she walked through the sitting room to the

top of the stairs, conscious of a nervous butterfly
sensation in her stomach, and something faintly
akin to anticipation tingling along her spine, as
she steeled herself to face her host and new
employer.

Whatever his aunt might privately think of
Jessica's presence, it was plain to Jessica that she
was a Spanish woman of the old school, and that
the will of the male members of her family was law.
She greeted Jessica pleasantly when she reached
the bottom of the stairs and explained that she
was waiting to show her the rest of the house,
'Which is rather rambling,' she told her, 'so I will
show you round so that you will not get lost.'

Jessica followed her into the main *sala*,
furnished with rare antiques, and with a silkily
beautiful and probably priceless Aubusson rug on
the floor. Beyond the windows lay a courtyard
similar in design to the one beneath Jessica's
tower, only this one was larger, encompassing
several formal beds of flowers, and whereas
Jessica's boasted a fountain and a small pool, this
one possessed a shimmeringly blue swimming
pool and a terrace.

'This is the main courtyard,' Sofia de
Calvadores told her. 'There are others, because
the Calvadores are first and foremost a Moorish
family and for many centuries strictly segregated
the differing sections of the family; privacy
becomes of prime importance when a house is
shared by several generations, and while this *sala*
and its courtyard has always been considered a
gathering place, there are several small, secluded
courtyards which in the past were the private
domain of various family members.'

'Just as the tower belonged to Rosalinda,' Jessica suggested. 'It must be fascinating to be able to trace one's family history back so far,' she added genuinely, suddenly remembering what Ramón Ferres had told them about the first Calvadores bride.

'Sometimes—sometimes it is not so pleasant to have the world privy to all one's secrets.'

'But the first Calvadores was one of Pedro the Cruel's knights, wasn't he?'

'Ah, you have heard that story,' Sofia smiled. 'Yes, indeed, that was so. He married the daughter of a Christian knight and it was for her, Rosalinda, that the tower was built.'

Jessica longed to question her further, but refrained, not wanting to appear too curious. What was it Ramón Ferres had said about the girl? That she had claimed her father's enemy had ravished her, and that rather than endure the taint of such an accusation he had married her?

'There you are!' a tiny voice suddenly piped up childishly, from the back of the room. 'Tio Sebastian sent me to look for you.'

'Lisa!' Señora Calvadores' voice reproached. 'Please remember we have a guest.' Her face relaxed into a faint smile as she turned to Jessica and explained in English, 'She is a little unthinking at times, and as always is excited by Sebastian's arrival. Lisa, come and meet Miss James, who is to work with Sebastian.'

A small, dark-haired child, with unexpectedly shadowed brown eyes, stepped forward and gravely offered her hand. She was immaculately if somewhat impractically dressed in a flounced white dress, matching ribbons securing her long hair, gleaming white socks and little black patent shoes such as Jessica couldn't remember seeing a little girl wearing since she herself had been a child.

She regarded Jessica with anxious gravity for several seconds and then burst out impetuously, 'Tio Sebastian won't be working all the time, will he?'

'Not quite,' Sebastian announced, startling Jessica with his silent entrance. 'You were so long, *pequeña*, I thought I should come and look for you.'

'Then, if you are not to work all the time, this afternoon we may go for a ride?' Lisa suggested with innocent coquetry. 'Please, Tio Sebastian! No one else lets me ride as fast as you.'

'We shall see, after lunch,' he told her. 'First your aunt must tell me if you have been a good girl while I have been gone.'

The child ran across to him, clinging to his arm while she assured him that indeed she had, and Jessica was shocked by the sudden wave of longing she experienced to be part of that charmed circle, with Sebastian's free arm securely round her.

The feeling was gone almost immediately, superseded by the knowledge that she was indulging in a ridiculous daydream, probably brought on by the fact that she was virtually alone in an alien land, excluded from the intimate family scene being played in front of her.

'Sebastian spoils her,' Sofia Calvadores complained as she and Jessica followed them out of the room, 'but in the circumstances it is easy to understand why. She is the image of her mother and . . .' She broke off as though feeling that she had said too much, drawing Jessica's attention to the doors leading to some of the other rooms as they walked into the hall.

'This is Sebastian's study,' she told her, opening one door and giving Jessica a brief glimpse of highly polished heavy furniture and a stained wooden floor covered in rich animal skins. 'But of course he will show you that himself later.'

The dining room seemed huge, the glittering chandeliers and frank opulence of the heavy mahogany table, polished until one could see one's reflection in it, making Jessica blink a little in dismay. She had forgotten how formal life could still be in the great Spanish houses.

'First an aperitif,' Sebastian announced, pouring small measures of golden sherry into small glasses and handing first his aunt and then Jessica one. 'This is made with the produce from our vines,' he told Jessica as she sipped hesitantly at the amber liquid. She had had nothing to eat all day and was beginning to feel the effects. A glass of sherry on an empty stomach was the last thing she wanted, but rather than cause offence by refusing she sipped hesitantly at the rich liquid. It slid warmly down her throat, but any hopes she had had of simply sipping a little and leaving the rest were dashed when Sebastian said ominously, 'Perhaps it is not to your liking?'

As though she would dare not like it! she thought half hysterically, and quickly drank the rest, and wishing she hadn't when her head started to spin muzzily.

It was still spinning when Sebastian indicated

that she should sit down at the table. A servant was holding her chair for her, and she walked hesitantly towards it, appalled to realise how disorientated the sherry had made her feel. Surely it was far more potent than anything she had drunk at home?

'Jessica!' Sebastian's voice cut sharply through her muddled thoughts.

'I ... it's ... I'm so sorry,' she managed to gasp as the world started whirling round dizzily and she reached for the first solid thing she could find, her fingers tightening convulsively on Sebastian's jacketed arm.

She heard him swear mildly, and then to her relief the mists started to clear.

'It was the sherry,' she managed to explain apologetically. 'I didn't have any breakfast, and ...'

'It is very potent if you are not used to it,' Sebastian's aunt agreed. 'Sebastian,' she directed her nephew, 'it is your fault for insisting she drink it, but you will feel better directly, my dear,' she comforted Jessica.

What a terrible impression she must be creating, Jessica thought with burning cheeks, and she released Sebastian's arm as though it were live coals. She didn't miss the flash of sardonic comprehension in his eyes and shrank back when he bent his head and murmured softly, 'You cling to me as fiercely as a dove to the branch that gives it shelter, but I am not deceived by your air of helpless dismay. Jorge told me of the wild beach barbecues you both attended, when drinking raw Sangria was the order of the day, so please do not expect me to believe that one single glass of sherry could have such a calamitous effect.'

What was he trying to imply? That she might have some other motive for clinging to him? But what?

'If you are having second thoughts,' he added, supplying her with the answer, 'and thinking that any man in your bed is better than none, do not, I beg you, even think of nominating me for the role. As I have already said, I am particular about with whom I share the pleasures of the act of love.'

'Tio Sebastian, what are you saying to Miss James?' Lisa piped up curiously. 'She is looking all pink and funny!'

His aunt quickly shushed the child, but not before Jessica had pulled away and slid into her chair. What must his aunt think of her? she wondered bitterly; or was she inured to her nephew's habits? Did she perhaps simply ignore the real role in his life of the women whom he brought home? They would think they were lovers, he had told her, and she was forced to admit that he had been right, but how did one correct such insidious suggestions? By simply and frankly correcting them? How could she tell his aunt they were not lovers? It was impossible!

After lunch Sebastian suggested that he should show her round the laboratory.

'Can I come too, Tio?' Lisa pleaded. 'I promise I will be good.'

'If you have no objection?' he murmured enquiringly to Jessica.

She shook her head. In truth she would be glad of the little girl's company, because her excited chatter broke the constrained atmosphere that stretched between them.

The laboratory was situated at the back of the *hacienda*, in what had originally been an immense stable block but which Sebastian explained to Jessica had been converted into garages and his laboratory.

The door was padlocked and bolted, and he told her as he unlocked it that because of the dyes and processes used he allowed no one apart from himself to enter the building.

'At the moment we are working on a new generation of dyes, almost entirely based on natural substances, but there is still some problem with the stabilising agent, although that should not take too long to sort out.'

'You are the only company I know that uses only natural dyes,' Jessica mentioned. 'It's quite rare, but of course that's why no other concern can match you for delicacy of colour.'

'This is so,' Sebastian agreed, 'and that is why the exact blending and stabilising of the various agents is a closely guarded secret. Indeed, I am the only person in the company who possesses the complete formula—it is as valuable as that to us.'

Jessica could well understand why. The subtlety and delicacy of their colours was one of the things that helped to make their range of fabrics so successful.

The laboratory was well equipped, and she followed with interest Sebastian's description of the work he was carrying out, although her prime interest lay not so much in the dying of the fabric but in the design of it.

There was an office off the laboratory with a row of metal filing cabinets, and Sebastian unlocked one, producing some detailed sketches and swatches of fabric which he handed to her.

'These are the colours we are hoping to produce for next season's fabrics—as you know, the Colour Council normally decide a season's colours two or three years in advance. These are the colours suggested by the last Council meeting. What we have to do now is to incorporate them into the design of the fabric. What I should like you to do initially is to work on them and produce some suggestions for me.'

Jessica nodded, excitement stirring as, against her will, she became fascinated by the project ahead. She did know that the Colour Council worked two years ahead of the fashion designers, selecting the spectrum of colours for a particular season, and the swatches Sebastian had handed her made her mouth water in anticipation. They were autumn and winter colours; black, charcoal grey, softly muted heathers and a bright peacock blue shading to mauve.

'You can use the office here, or the sitting room in the tower, whichever you wish,' Sebastian told her carelessly, glancing down at Lisa as she tugged impatiently at his hand.

'You said we could go riding,' she reminded him, pouting a little. 'You promised!'

'You are forgetting that we have a guest,' Sebastian reminded her firmly. 'Would it not be polite also to ask Miss James if she would care to come with us?'

The question was for Lisa's benefit and not hers, Jessica acknowledged. Like other Latin races Spanish children were petted and indulged, but good manners were considered paramount. Hesitantly Lisa asked if she would like to join them, her relief patent and winning Jessica a wide relieved smile, when she gently refused.

'I'll take these up to the tower with me,' she told Sebastian, adding to Lisa, 'Enjoy your ride.'

She didn't go straight back to the tower, but found her way instead to the small enclosed courtyard she could see from her bedroom window. Jacaranda bloomed profusely against the walls, mingling with the bougainvillea, while two doves cooed melodiously on the rim of the pool. The courtyard had a secluded, mysterious air, as though it preferred moonlight and the seductive whispers of lovers to sunshine and birdsong. Had Rosalinda ever walked here with a lover—the husband who had married her so unwillingly, perhaps? Had they ever found love together?

When she returned to the house she met Sebastian's aunt in the hall. 'Lisa and Sebastian are going riding,' she told her, adding impulsively, 'Lisa is a delightful child.'

'Charming—when she wants to be,' Sofia Calvadores agreed dryly, 'but Sebastian spoils her. It is natural, I suppose. He is all she has.'

'Her parents are dead, then?' Jessica asked sympathetically.

Was it her imagination or did the Señora hesitate briefly before saying, 'Yes, I'm afraid so, she is Sebastian's ward. It could be difficult for her should Sebastian marry and have children of his own.'

'But surely, when he does, his wife will

understand and accept that Lisa is bound to find it hard at first,' Jessica suggested.

Señora Calvadores smiled. 'One would hope so, but it would depend very much on the wife. Sebastian must marry, of course, to carry on the name. He was betrothed once, but his betrothed died—a tragic accident in a car.' She sighed and shook her head. 'It was all a long time ago, and best forgotten now.'

It was late afternoon before Lisa and Sebastian returned to the *hacienda*. Jessica had been working in her sitting room when a maid had knocked and told her that it was the custom for the ladies of the household to drink sherry and eat almond pastries at this particular time of the day, adding that Señora Calvadores was waiting for her in the main courtyard.

She hadn't realised how cramped her limbs had become, and she was still a little stiff when she emerged into the sunshine to find that Lisa and Sebastian had returned and were sitting with the Señora.

Sebastian moved and Jessica realised there was someone else with them; a tall stately woman in her early thirties, her thick dark hair drawn back in a chignon, her cold dark eyes appraising Jessica as they moved over her.

Jessica recognised her from the hotel in Seville, and wondered who she was.

'Ah, Jessica, there you are. Allow me to introduce Miss James to you, *cara*,' he said to his companion. 'She has come here to work for me for several weeks.'

'I hope she realises her good fortune,' was the brunette's acid response.

'Jessica—Pilar Sanchez, a close friend and neighbour of ours.'

'Merely a close friend,' Pilar pouted, slanting Jessica another acid glance. 'Come, our relationship is stronger than that. If poor Manuela had lived we would have been brother and sister.' Scarlet-tipped fingers lay provocatively along Sebastian's forearm, the look in her eyes as she gazed up at him anything but sisterly. There was a strange aching sensation in Jessica's stomach. They could be lovers. *Were* they lovers? Surely not; Pilar obviously came from a family as exalted as Sebastian's own; her sister had obviously been engaged to him. If he needed a wife surely he need look no further than Pilar. Or was there perhaps some bar on such a marriage because of his relationship with her sister? Jessica wasn't sure about the Catholic church's ruling on such things.

She was brought back to her surroundings with a jolt as Pilar scolded sharply, temper flags flying scarlet in her cheeks, 'Lisa, your fingers—don't touch my dress, child, you will ruin it!'

The little girl's face crumpled. She looked uncertainly at Sebastian, who was frowning, and then towards his aunt, who said gently, 'Lisa, go and find Maria. It is time for you to rest.'

'Really, Sebastian, that child is growing impossible!' Pilar commented sharply when Lisa had gone. 'You should send her to a convent where she could learn obedience.'

'As Manuela did?' Sebastian drawled sardonically, but Jessica couldn't understand the expression in Sofia's eyes or the reason for his aunt's suddenly tense body.

Jessica had to wait until after dinner to show Sebastian the work she had done during the day. To her surprise he didn't criticise it as thoroughly as she had anticipated, instead showing her some work he had done himself.

'Initially I didn't want to give you any guidelines,' he told her, 'because it is important that we work on the same wavelength. What you have done shows me that you have a natural sympathy for our fabrics and what we hope to achieve with them. Tomorrow we shall spend an hour together in my study talking about what line the new range will take. You like the tower?' he asked her unexpectedly.

Caught off guard by the absence of his normal cynicism and contempt, Jessica replied enthusiastically, 'I love it, but I can't help wondering if Rosalinda was happy there. She occupied those rooms alone . . .'

'Instead of sharing those of her husband?' Sebastian interrupted. 'This is true, but it was only in the initial days that she occupied the tower. You have obviously heard the story and you must remember that she had accused her husband of seducing her, when in fact he knew he had not. He had married her to protect his good name, but he swore he would remain celibate rather than touch an unwilling woman who had already given herself to another. So matters might have continued if Rosalinda hadn't found the courage to go to him and confess that she had lied to her father, but not to conceal any affair with another man, simply because she had fallen desperately in love with Rodriguez, and wanted him for her husband, but she knew that because

of the enmity that existed between him and her
father she had no chance of marrying him. So she
conceived her plan. She knew of the pride of both
Rodriguez and her father and knew that if she
were to accuse Rodriguez of dishonouring her he
would be forced to make reparation. It was a bold
step to take; she had to face dishonour herself—
admit to her lack of chastity, perhaps endure the
hatred of her husband for ever, when he knew
how he had been tricked.

'But Rosalinda was beautiful as well as bold.
Rodriguez could not resist her tears of contrition
for the trick she had played, and she told him that
she was still a virgin. She did not spend many
nights alone in her tower,' Sebastian added dryly.

'So she tricked him into marriage, just as
you've accused me of trying to trick Jorge,'
Jessica pointed out.

He looked at her angrily. 'The two cases are
entirely different. She was motivated by love,
which excuses much; you are motivated by
material greed, which is unforgivable.'

Why was it that no matter what subject they
discussed they always ended up quarrelling?
Jessica wondered tiredly as she gathered together
her designs and the swatches of fabric.

'You are looking pale,' Sebastian confounded
her by saying abruptly. 'My aunt tells me you
worked all afternoon and then into the evening.'

'You had a guest,' Jessica pointed out, without
reminding him that Pilar had looked anything but
pleased at his suggestion that she stay with them.
'And besides, I enjoyed it.'

'In future you will take proper exercise.' He
frowned. 'Can you ride?' Jessica shook her head.

'A pity, you could have joined Lisa when she rides with me in the morning.'

He made her sound like another child to be humoured and scolded, Jessica thought wryly.

'I can walk, or swim,' she told him. 'And besides, the sooner the work is completed the sooner I can leave.'

For some reason his mouth compressed angrily at that statement, and with one of those quickly shifting moods she was coming to dread Jessica felt a frisson of awareness steal through her. He had discarded his jacket, and the breeze from the open windows flattened his shirt tautly to his body, moulding the muscled power of his torso. His shirt was open at the neck, the pale glimmer of the white fabric emphasising the darkness of his skin. A pulse beat steadily at the base of his throat, drawing her eyes, a curious sensual tension enveloping her. She moistened her lips and watched as he moved slowly towards her.

'Jessica . . .' He broke off as the *sala* door was suddenly thrust open and a tall young man with a shock of dark hair and a mobile mouth hurried in, coming to a standstill as he saw Jessica.

'Jorge!' Sebastian exclaimed in surprise. '*Dios!* What are you doing here?'

Jorge! Jessica stared in disbelief at the newcomer. This was Sebastian's brother?

It was plain that he was slightly taken aback by Sebastian's attitude. He glanced uncertainly first at his brother and then at Jessica.

'I wanted to see you,' he said in a puzzled voice. 'I had no idea you were planning to come here. You never mentioned it when we spoke on the telephone.'

'Perhaps because I had no idea you were intending your stay with the Reajons to be of such a short duration. It was, I believe, to be for one month.'

Jessica felt sorry for the younger man as he flushed and looked uncomfortable. 'That is one of the things I wanted to talk to you about, Sebastian. I . . .' He broke off and glanced hesitantly at Jessica, then turned to his brother, saying gallantly, 'But you have a guest—and a very beautiful one. Aren't you going to introduce me?'

To say that Sebastian looked stupefied was an overstatement, but there was a certain amount of shock as he registered the words. He too turned to look at Jessica, and she quailed beneath the message she read in his eyes.

'I thought Miss James was already known to you,' he said in icy tones. 'In fact to such an extent it is not so long ago that you were pleading with me to help you remove her from your life.'

Jessica felt sorry for the young man when he flushed again, but it was obvious to her that Sebastian intended to spare her nothing.

'I am Isabel's cousin,' she explained to Jorge, ignoring Sebastian. 'There's been a slight misunderstanding and your brother mistook me for Isabel. When I learned what he had to say to her I decided not to enlighten him. For all her faults, Isabel is acutely sensitive . . .'

She didn't need to say any more. Jorge looked appalled, and turned horrified eyes on his brother. 'Sebastian, you said nothing about speaking personally to Isabel! We were agreed that a letter . . .'

'So we were, but then I had no idea that she intended to come and plead her case personally—or so I thought. Naturally my first priority was to protect you.'

'Another misconception on your part,' Jessica told him bitterly. 'Isabel ... didn't tell me the full facts. She was terrified that you intended to go to England to see her. She is now engaged to someone else ... and quite naturally ...' She was beginning to flounder, not wanting to betray Isabel's stupidity and lack of moral fibre, but Sebastian, it seemed, had no such qualms.

'What you are saying is that your cousin lied to you.'

'Not deliberately,' Jessica hastened to defend Isabel. 'She simply wanted to make sure there would be no repercussions from her letter to Jorge—written when she was feeling extremely worried and almost desperate. She wanted me to tell Jorge that she fully accepted that their liaison was at an end.'

It wasn't quite the truth, but it would suffice.

'You knew I had mistaken you for her, why did you not tell me the truth then?' Sebastian demanded, watching her with narrowed eyes.

'Because I didn't want to expose Isabel to the same sort of insults I had been forced to endure myself,' Jessica told him coolly. 'Just as you wanted to protect your brother, I wanted to protect my cousin!'

'We will speak of this later,' he told her silkily. 'For now ...'

'You naturally want to be alone with your brother,' Jessica supplied dryly, not adding that she was more than happy to leave them alone together.

Jorge's unexpected arrival had given her a bad shock. Whereas she ought to be experiencing relief and satisfaction that Sebastian now knew the truth, all she could think was that he might now send her back to England, and for some reason she didn't wait to analyse too carefully, she didn't want to go!

CHAPTER SIX

'AH, there you are, I hope you will permit me to join you?'

Jessica glanced at Jorge's concerned face and smiled. She was sitting in her small courtyard, working on some of the designs, and enjoying the sunshine.

'Sebastian is working in his laboratory,' Jorge informed her, needlessly, since Sebastian himself had told her at breakfast that he could be found there should she want him. There had also been a look in his eyes that told her that there was still a reckoning to come, but that was something she was refusing to think about!

'I must apologise, for my . . . for my brother's behaviour,' Jorge managed at last, flushing a little. 'It is unforgivable that he should have involved you in this affair.' He bit his lip. 'He has given me the gist of what has happened between you, although why, feeling as he does, he has brought you here to the *hacienda* to work for him I do not know!'

He looked perplexed and unhappy, but Jessica didn't enlighten him. He might think Sebastian had told him the truth, but she knew differently.

'I was speaking to my aunt this morning and she seems to think . . . that is, Sebastian has given her the impression . . . that . . . that you are lovers,' he added uncomfortably, 'and yet plainly this is not so. I shall speak to him about it on your behalf. Isabel talked of you to me, I know you are not . . . that you do not . . .'

'That I'm not promiscuous?' Jessica supplied dryly, privately suspecting that Isabel had been far more unflattering in her description of her, but Jorge seized on the expression gratefully.

'*Si*,' he agreed, 'this is so . . . Sebastian cannot appreciate what my aunt thinks, for he would never expose a young woman of unblemished reputation to such an insult.'

Heavens, he sounded like something out of a Victorian novel! Jessica thought to herself. Surely he couldn't be serious? But apparently he was.

'I shall speak to him about it,' he added again. 'It is not right.'

Right or wrong, she couldn't see Sebastian being easily influenced by his younger brother, Jessica reflected when Jorge had gone.

She had been on her own for about half an hour when she glanced up, hearing footsteps coming in her direction. To her surprise she saw Pilaı coming towards her, the older woman's mouth grimly compressed, two bright coins of colour burning in her otherwise completely pale face.

'You are wasting your time!' she hissed to Jessica without preamble. 'Sebastian does not really want you. He has only ever loved one woman—my sister, and . . .'

Jessica tried to interrupt, to assure her companion that she had no romantic interest in Sebastian. Something about the way the older woman was watching her triggered alarm bells in her mind. It struck her that there was something driven, something almost bordering on hysteria, in Pilar's manner.

'He was obsessed by her,' Pilar continued almost as though Jessica wasn't there, 'but one day he will have to marry, if only in order to have sons, and who better than the sister of the woman he loved?'

'But surely ...' Surely there is Jorge, Jessica had been about to say, but once again Pilar didn't give her the opportunity to finish.

'You are thinking of Lisa,' she said bitterly, 'but she is only a daughter. Sebastian needs sons.'

Lisa was Sebastian's daughter? Shock coursed through Jessica, stingingly, followed by a hot, molten anger. How dared he question her morals when he ...

'You didn't know?' Pilar started to laugh wildly. 'Of course he wouldn't tell you. No one is supposed to know about it. My sister Manuela had been his *novia* for many months and the preparations for the wedding were all in hand when she suddenly became ill. It was the strain of preparing for the wedding, our doctor told my parents, and Manuela was sent to Argentina to stay with relatives there. When she returned it was obvious that there was to be a child—Sebastian's child. My parents were bitterly hurt and shocked. Sebastian whom they trusted and treated like a son had taken Manuela's innocence before they were married. Preparations for the ceremony were speeded up. My mother begged Manuela to tell her why she had not confided in her before her visit to Argentina. I myself was married then. I too was shocked by Sebastian's behaviour, but I knew how much he loved her.

And then just two days before the ceremony Manuela asked me if she could borrow my car.' Pilar hesitated and for a moment there was a sly, almost gloating expression in her eyes.

'She was involved in an accident near Seville, and was taken immediately to the hospital. They were able to save the child, but by the time Sebastian reached the hospital Manuela was dead.'

Jessica couldn't conceal her shock and distaste. Poor Manuela! By all accounts she had been tragically innocent and young, and now she was dead and Sebastian was left only with memories of what might have been, and a child—his child! Why then had she been introduced as his 'ward'?

'Of course everything was hushed up,' Pilar continued. 'Only the closest members of the family know of the circumstances of Lisa's birth.' Her lips twisted, and Jessica was reminded of how much she seemed to dislike the little girl—a child who was after all her niece. 'Lisa is a constant reminder to Sebastian of my sister,' Pilar continued, and with a flash of insight Jessica realised that Pilar was jealous; jealous of her sister's child.

'It was a tragic year for our family,' she added. 'First Manuela and then my own husband and parents were killed when my husband was taking them to Minorca in his plane, but worst of all— Lisa.' She shuddered. 'It is just as well Manuela died. Had she lived she would have been shunned for her sin.'

Jessica could hardly believe her ears. What Pilar was saying was positively feudal—and what of Sebastian, surely he was equally to blame, if indeed 'blame' was the word. And poor Lisa! She obviously didn't realise that Sebastian was her father. Jessica felt an upsurge of anger against him. How could he deny his daughter her right to her relationship with him? Pilar said he had loved Manuela, but in Jessica's opinion it was a poor sort of love that denied the human evidence of that love.

She was still trying to come to terms with what Pilar had told her after lunch, when Sebastian announced that he wanted to talk to Jorge in his study.

Lisa was at a loose end, and asked Jessica if she could sit with her. 'I will be very good,' she promised, 'but it is Tia Sofia's day for having her friends round, and it is very dull.'

Jessica was touched that the little girl should want her company. Her work on the designs was well advanced, and in fact she could do little until she had spoken to Sebastian, so she suggested instead that Lisa show her round the environs of the *hacienda*.

The little girl was an entertaining companion. Jessica had always liked children, and concealed her pity carefully when Lisa commented on how lonely she sometimes felt.

'Pilar wants to send me away,' she confided fearfully, 'but Tio Sebastian will not let her.'

How could Sebastian deny his relationship with his child?

It was late afternoon when they returned. Sebastian's aunt was in the *sala* with her friends, and Lisa politely listened to their questions, responding demurely, quite different from the exuberant child she had been when she had been with Jessica.

Jessica could tell that she herself was the subject of a good deal of discreet curiosity.

'Jessica is a particular friend of Sebastian's,' his aunt explained.

'But I understand from my niece that you were here primarily to work for him,' one formidable matron said icily.

Jessica wasn't surprised to discover that she was Pilar's aunt. 'And your family don't mind?' she asked, apparently unable to believe it when Jessica assured her that they didn't. 'In Spain no young woman of good family would be permitted to stay in the home of an unmarried man without a female relative with her.'

'I am here to work,' Jessica reminded her coolly, uneasily reminded of what Jorge had said. Did these women think she was Sebastian's mistress? What did it matter if they did? And yet it was an uncomfortable sensation to have them studying her, perhaps talking about her when she wasn't there.

After they left the *sala*, Jessica went upstairs to her tower, while Lisa was whisked away by her maid for a rest.

The household ran like clockwork, and yet apparently without any effort on the part of Sebastian's aunt, although Jessica had noticed that the staff consulted her every day just after breakfast. It must be an enormous responsibility caring for the valuable antiques and art treasures that filled the *hacienda*, and she reflected that it was impossible not to admire the selflessness of

Spanish women when it came to devoting themselves to their homes.

She had wanted to see Sebastian about the designs she was working on and gathering up her work she went downstairs to his study. She could hear voices from inside, one of them recognisably Jorge's and bitterly defensive.

Now was obviously not the time to intrude, and she was just walking away when Rafael, the major-domo of the household, appeared.

'I was hoping to have a word with the Conde,' Jessica explained in response to his unspoken question, 'but . . .'

'I shall inform him when he is free,' Rafael assured her. 'Perhaps you would care for a tray of tea? In the past our English guests have often asked for tea at this time.'

It was six o'clock and as Jessica knew from experience, it would be several hours before they dined. Spaniards dined late, so she thanked Rafael and told him that tea would indeed be most welcome.

It arrived twenty minutes later—a bone china tea service and a plate of delicate almond cakes. Until she saw them Jessica hadn't realised how hungry she felt. She had just finished her second cup of tea when someone knocked briskly on the door. She knew without opening it, with some instinctive sixth sense, that it was Sebastian.

He looked preoccupied and bleakly angry, and her heart sank. Now was obviously not the time to discuss her ideas with him.

'Now,' he said, when he had closed the door with a precision that sent shivers of alarm feathering along her spine, 'perhaps you will be good enough to explain why you did not tell me the truth about your cousin?'

He was leaning against the door, arms folded across his chest, unconsciously straining the fabric, his eyes glinting metallic grey as they waited for her response.

'I've already told you,' Jessica said tightly. She had forgotten the implicit threat she had seen in his eyes when Jorge unwittingly revealed the truth, in the shock of listening to Pilar's disclosures.

'I wanted to protect Isabel . . .'

'Protect her, or her engagement?' he asked with devastating insight. 'Jorge has told me of this John—apparently she was contemplating becoming engaged to him when she met Jorge.'

'Jorge was simply a holiday romance,' Jessica told him firmly. 'Isabel is silly but not venal. I can assure you she had no mercenary interest in Jorge.'

'No? Then why did she threaten him with this child she says she conceived?'

'A mistake,' Jessica told him. 'Surely you can appreciate her position? She came back from holiday, and then discovered that she might be carrying Jorge's child, or so she thought, so she panicked . . .'

'And tried to force him into marrying her,' Sebastian concluded distastefully. 'And this is the innocent child you wished to protect? No, I cannot accept it.'

She wasn't going to tell him how Isabel had lied to her, Jessica decided angrily, her chin tilting defiantly as she stared up at him.

'It doesn't matter to me whether you do or not,' she told him unsteadily. 'All I want to do now is to put the entire incident behind me.'

It wasn't completely true—certain aspects of it would remain to haunt her always, and she was very much afraid that what she felt for Sebastian came dangerously close to love. Quite how or why it should have happened she didn't know, but these last few days had underlined, time and time again, that she was far from indifferent to him. She only had to register the way her pulses raced whenever he walked in a room to be aware of that! And yet he was the complete antithesis of all she admired in men. Arrogant, domineering and apparently incapable of facing up to his responsibilities.

'Easier said than done.' He frowned, unfolding his arms, and moved silently to the window. 'As Jorge has just been at considerable pains to point out to me, my aunt, and no doubt by this time, her cronies, all believe you to be my mistress.'

He seemed to be waiting for some response, and Jessica refused to acknowledge the hurting shaft of pain his indifference occasioned.

'We know differently,' she told him. 'And besides, the opinion of half a dozen or so people I've never set eyes on before and am not likely to see again doesn't trouble me.'

'I'm sure it doesn't,' Sebastian agreed grittily, 'but unfortunately, I do have to see them again and it does concern me, as everything touching upon the good name of our family must.'

It was on the tip of Jessica's tongue to tell him that this was something he should have thought of before, but instead she said unsteadily, 'Yes, I see that having a reputation such as yours must be a great burden to so proud a man.'

Instantly she realised she had gone too far. Fingers like talons gripped her wrist.

'Just what do you mean by that?' he demanded softly.

'I think you know,' Jessica managed bravely. 'There's Lisa, and people are not blind . . .'

'Ah, someone has told you about Manuela,' he said comprehensively, his mouth twisting in a cynically bitter smile. 'And of course you are quite right. There is endless gossip about Lisa, and her parenthood, and because of that I have to be extremely circumspect—for her sake as much as my own.'

'I can't see why you don't tell her the truth,' Jessica told him huskily. 'It's cruel not to do. She's bound to find out.'

'You are very concerned on her behalf.' Again the mockingly cynical smile.

'Because I happen to like her; and because also I know what it's like to lose both parents, and nothing, but nothing compensates for that loss. Any parent is better than none at all,' she told him fiercely, 'and you're depriving her of the right to that relationship.'

'Enough!' With a ferocity that jerked the breath from her lungs she was dragged towards him. 'I will not listen to any more. You will be silent!'

'How will you make me?' Jessica demanded breathlessly. 'By flinging me in your dungeons?'

'Oh no.' The soft way he spoke, and the insolently appraising look that accompanied the words, sent nervous tremors of warning chasing down her spine. 'Like this!'

He moved so suddenly that she couldn't evade

him, hard fingers tangling in her hair and tugging painfully until she thought her spine would crack under the pressure. His eyes searched her vulnerable, exposed features in silence, while hers spat the defiance she now dared not voice.

'It is too late for obedience now,' he told her silkily. 'You must take your punishment.'

His mouth on hers was brutally chastising, his fingers forcefully gripping her waist, a savage anger that she had not seen before burning in the pressure of his mouth against hers.

She felt frozen and completely unable to feel, her eyes glazing as she tried not to mind that he was humiliating her like this, turning what should be a sensually exciting experience into a deeply humiliating one.

As though he sensed that somehow she had escaped his vengeance, the pressure of his mouth suddenly softened and then shockingly his lips left hers, his tongue slowly tracing their quivering outline, until she ached and yearned for the feel of his mouth. The anger had gone from his eyes, to be replaced by a slumbrous heat.

Her body seemed to melt against him entirely without her consent, her eyes closing as he feathered light kisses over the trembling lids.

'*Por Dios*,' he muttered hoarsely against her ear, 'there is a chemistry between us that refuses to be denied!'

Jessica knew she should make some protest, tell him to release her, but his fingers were stroking soothingly along her scalp, his mouth investigating the exposed vulnerability of her throat, releasing a fluttering fever of sensations that made her long only to cling to the breadth of his shoulders, and offer herself up to whatever he wanted from her.

Not even the heat of his fingers scorching the curves of her breasts had the power to alarm her. Instead she felt an elemental response to the caress, coupled with a primitive need to feel his touch against her skin without the constricting barrier of clothes. As though somehow her thoughts communicated themselves to him, Jessica heard him groan and saw with surprise the dark flush mantling his skin and the heated glitter of his gaze.

She made no attempt to stop him when he unbuttoned her blouse and slid it from her shoulders. Her lacy bra emphasised rather than concealed the curves of her breasts and her pulses seemed to quicken in elemental excitement as Sebastian's dark gaze lingered on the pale almost translucent skin.

'How much more attractive is this than the over-exposed bronzed bodies that litter our beaches! This,' he added emotively, stroking a finger over the pale flesh, 'is an enticement to man to touch and taste. The very paleness of your skin hints at a chastity that arouses the hunter in man, no matter how false that impression might be.'

Jessica gasped as he released the catch of her bra, exposing her breasts fully to his gaze. She knew she should feel shame; yet what she did feel was a tremulous, aching excitement; a need to have him touch her. As though he guessed her thoughts his hands cupped her breasts, her nipples hardening devastatingly at his touch. The stroke of his thumbs over the sensitised and aroused flesh incited a need to writhe and press herself close to his body, the husky moan torn from her throat shocking her with it sensuality.

'*Dios*, I despise myself for it, but right now I want nothing as much as I want to take you to bed, to feel your silkiness against my skin, like a soothing balm to overheated flesh. I want to lose myself in your softness . . . I . . . What is it about you that makes me forget what you are?' Sebastian muttered huskily, lifting her in his arms, his eyes moving from her face to the rosy peaks of her breasts and then back again.

She shouldn't be letting him do this, Jessica thought distractedly, but every nerve centre in her body was screaming for the satisfaction she knew only he could give. She felt the bed give under their combined weight, and all her muscles tightened in stunned protest as his mouth moved hungrily over the curve of one breast, the rough stroke of his tongue against the aching nipple causing her stomach muscles to lock in mute protest at the waves of pleasure crashing down on her, teaching her more about sensuality and her own body's response to it in two minutes than she had learned in twenty-odd years.

'*Dios*, I want you!'

He was only echoing her own thoughts, her own need. She had never felt this overpowering desire to know a man's possession before, and it shocked her that she should now. But then she had never loved a man as she loved Sebastian.

Loved! With sickening certainty she knew that it was too late to banish the treacherous and insidious truth. She *did* love him.

'Jessica?'

He was watching her, studying the flushed contours of her face, the arousal she felt sure must be there. She longed to touch him as intimately as he was touching her, and she reached out tentatively towards him, her fingers trembling as they encountered the rigidity of his collarbone.

'*Dios*, I have hungered for your touch against my skin,' he told her huskily, burying his mouth in the curve of her shoulder, 'almost from the very first. It is true, is it not, that there was a vital chemistry between us—a desire that neither of us can deny.'

Jessica wanted to say that it was not purely desire that motivated her, but Sebastian was wrenching open his shirt and her eyes were drawn to the naked virility of his body. Without the trappings of civilisation, the expensive suit and the silk shirt, his body was totally male, tautly muscled, his chest shadowed with dark body hair that tapered towards his waist.

'*Dios*, Sebastian, what is the meaning of this!'

They were so engrossed in one another that neither of them had heard the door open. Jessica's shocked eyes saw his aunt's disturbed face and behind her Pilar's glitteringly triumphant one.

'I told you you were wrong,' Pilar said triumphantly. 'I told you they were lovers!'

Sebastian was shielding Jessica with his body, but that didn't stop the shame coursing through her, burning into her soul as she realised how they must appear to their onlookers.

'Sebastian!' his aunt's voice was deeply reproachful. 'I am wounded beyond words that you would use your home as . . .'

'That is enough.' Quietly and calmly Sebastian silenced both women. 'If you will wait in the sitting room, there is something I must say to you both.'

He waited until they had gone and then quickly stood up, his back to Jessica.

'My apologies for that,' he told her curtly. 'I never imagined that . . .'

That what? Jessica wondered. That he would allow his desire to overrule his dislike of her as a person?

'I must speak with my aunt.'

He was gone, closing the door behind him, leaving Jessica to bitterly regret giving in to the wild clamouring tide of desire he had aroused in her. How on earth could she face his aunt or Pilar again? She felt humiliated beyond bearing that they should have witnessed such intimacies. She had wanted to give herself in love, but somehow their interruption had reduced her to the status of a kept plaything, whose only role was to satisfy the needs of her master who might enjoy her body while openly despising her mind.

'Jessica, could you give us a moment?' The quiet voice suggested that if she didn't he would come in and get her.

What was he going to say to her? she wondered nervously, checking in the mirror that she was properly dressed, before screwing up her courage and walking nervously into the other room.

From Sebastian's aunt she received a kind if somewhat sorrowful look. From Pilar she received one of blazing hatred.

'You cannot mean this, Sebastian,' she was saying as Jessica walked into the room. 'It is total folly!'

'That is something only I can decide,' Sebastian replied with iron inflexibility. 'I have just told my aunt and Pilar that we are to be married,' he told Jessica coolly, his eyes warning her against saying anything to contradict his statement. 'As Pilar and Jorge have pointed out to me, I have already been responsible for the destruction of one girl's good name. I will not have the Calvadores name dragged in the mud a second time.'

'But, Sebastian, to go to these lengths!' Pilar protested, glaring at Jessica. 'It is not necessary. You have only to send the girl away. Nothing will be said.'

'No, Sebastian is right,' his aunt interrupted firmly. 'You must not try to dissuade him, Pilar. Jessica, I am pleased to welcome you to our family.' She walked across to Jessica, grasping her hands, kissing her gently on either cheek. 'Come Pilar, it is time we left. Sebastian, if you will tell me what arrangements I am to make . . .'

'If he does intend to marry her he will want it done as quietly and quickly as possible,' Pilar said spitefully. 'He will not want another bride giving birth before he can get her to the altar!'

'Enough!'

Jessica quailed at the fury in Sebastian's voice, but Pilar seemed not to mind, merely shrugging insolently as she looked at Jessica. 'He may marry you,' she told her, 'but always you will know why. Can you live with that?'

She was right, Jessica thought as they left the room and Sebastian closed the door. Of course she could not marry him. And yet he had admitted that he desired her, surely from that something might grow? His family was one that for generations had endured arranged marriages, marriages with far less hope of success than theirs, and surely she had enough love for them both?

All these were wild and foolish thoughts, she admitted as Sebastian turned and she saw the bleak anger in his eyes.

'We don't really have to get married,' she faltered. 'I can leave . . .'

'And have everyone know that once again a Calvadores has betrayed his name?' he said bitterly. 'Never! I cannot believe that marriage to me will be so abhorrent to you. Sexually we are compatible,' he gave her a thin smile. 'At least we will not be bored in bed, and as for the rest,' he shrugged, 'I shall have my work, and please God eventually you will have our children.'

Why, when he said it like that, did it sound such a barren existence, so different from the one she had visualised?

'I should have listened to Jorge and not given into my need to feel the softness of your skin beneath my hands,' he added bitterly. 'We will be married just as quickly as it can be arranged, do you agree?'

Jessica wanted to say 'no'. She should say 'no', but it was a weak, hesitant 'yes' that finally left her lips, earning her a look of burning contempt.

'A wise decision. You will be the first Calvadores bride in nearly a thousand years of history who has not come to her marriage bed a virgin.'

'You once told me you would never marry a woman who had known other lovers,' Jessica reminded him with a dry throat, wondering if now he would change his mind.

'Circumstances sometimes dictate a lowering of one's standards. If I do not marry you now, doubtless I will be accused of despoiling two innocent young women.' His mouth twisted bitterly. 'I cannot allow that to happen, for the sake of my aunt and brother, if not for myself.'

'It's rather a high price to pay for family pride, isn't it?' Jessica queried numbly. Never in her wildest imaginings had she ever imagined herself in a situation such as this.

'For some things no price is too high,' he told her sombrely, 'and when we celebrate the birth of our first son perhaps I will be able to tell myself that there is after all some virtue in our marriage.'

She would never allow a child of hers to be brought up thinking that his whole life must be given over to upholding the pride of the Calvadores name, Jessica decided fiercely. Her child would not be sad and lonely like Lisa. Her child . . .

With a shock she realised that already she was thinking about bearing Sebastian's child, and she knew then that she would marry him, no matter how much common sense warned her against it.

CHAPTER SEVEN

THREE days later they were married in Seville. Sebastian had asked Jessica, with the same distant politeness he had adopted towards her ever since she had accepted his proposal, if there was anyone she wanted to invite to the ceremony.

She thought fleetingly of her aunt and uncle and Colin, and then regretfully shook her head. To invite them would lead to too many questions; too many doubts to add to those already crowding her mind. It would be far easier to simply tell them once it was over.

Over! She was viewing the thought of her marriage in much the same light as she would a trip to the dentist, and who was to blame? Ever since the afternoon she had agreed to marry Sebastian their marriage had been treated as though it were an unpleasant necessity. It was true that Lisa had greeted the news with unalloyed joy.

'I'm so glad you're going to marry Tio Sebastian,' she had confided Jessica only that morning. 'I would have hated it if he had married Pilar. She doesn't like me!'

But as far as the rest of the family were concerned, it had been all long faces and grave expressions.

Jorge had sought Jessica out and confided that he could not see what other course his brother could have taken.

'He should never have allowed you to become the object of Pilar's speculation in the first place,' he had told her. 'Sebastian knows how possessive Pilar is about him, how she would seek to discredit anyone who is close to him.'

Jessica scarcely felt that she came into that category, and if that had been the reason for Pilar bursting in on them in the manner she had, it had had completely the opposite effect from the one she had desired.

She glanced briefly at Sebastian, wondering what thoughts lay behind the shuttered face. They had been married this morning, she was now the Condesa de Calvadores. She touched the new band of gold on her finger, as though the touch of the shiny metal would make her new status more real.

A wedding breakfast had been arranged at Calvadores town house. Fifty-odd guests had been invited—all close family, Sebastian's aunt had assured her, and all of whom would be bitterly resentful if they were not invited.

'They look upon Sebastian as the head of our family,' she had explained to Jessica when she had protested. 'It will only cause problems later if they are not invited. There has already been so much turmoil in his life . . .'

She broke off, and Jessica sensed that she was thinking back to that other girl Sebastian should have married. In fact Sofia had done all she could to welcome Jessica into the family, her serene expression betraying no hint of the shocked reproach Jessica had glimpsed in her eyes in those few horrifying seconds when she had followed Pilar into the tower room.

Only this morning as Jessica was dressing for the service she had come into her room, proffering a pearl choker.

'You must wear them,' she had insisted. 'Every Caldvadores bride does.'

'But I'm scarcely the bride you can have wanted for your nephew,' Jessica had protested miserably. Today of all days she longed to have her aunt with her, longed for the misty white dress she had always secretly dreamed of wearing, instead of the expensive silk separates she had bought hurriedly in Seville—extremely beautiful in their way, but scarcely bride-like.

'You love him,' Sofia had stunned Jessica by saying quietly, 'and that is enough for me. Above all else Sebastian is a man who needs a wife's love. I know he can sometimes seem hard, arrogant even,' a small smile lifted her mouth. 'My own husband was much the same, it is a Calvadores trait, unfortunately, but Sebastian has had to endure much in his life. The loss of his parents was a terrible blow to him. He had to assume the role of guardian and mentor to Jorge; and then there was poor Manuela. So much misery and pain! I have hoped for a long time to see him married. You will make him a good wife, I know, because you love him.'

'But he doesn't love me!' Jessica hadn't been able to stem the anguished words.

'He desires you, who knows where that desire may lead?'

Who knew indeed? Jessica thought unhappily, glancing down the length of the table, listening half-heartedly to the hushed Spanish voices. She was a part of this family now, an important part, as one dowager had already reminded her, for she would be the mother of the next head of the family.

They were not having a honeymoon; Sebastian had deemed it unnecessary. They would return to the *hacienda*, at least for a few weeks, until he had completed his work on the designs, and then they would divide their time between the house in Seville and the *hacienda*.

Out of the corner of her eye she noticed Jorge. Sebastian was angry with him because Jorge had announced that he would not marry Barbara.

'Isn't it enough that one of us has married without love?' he had flung at Sebastian in the middle of their argument, and Jessica, who had been standing outside the study waiting to talk to Sebastian, had fled, just managing to reach the privacy of her room before she dissolved in tears.

What sort of marriage had she commited herself to? One where her husband took his pleasure of her body while ignoring her mind? Could she endure that?

The breakfast seemed unending, her head throbbing with the rich food and drink, her body aching with a bone-jarring tension that made her jerk away from Sebastian when he rose, to cup her elbow, when they eventually left.

'*Dios*,' he swore, his eyes darkening to graphite, 'why do you shrink from me like a petrified virgin?'

Because that's exactly what I am, Jessica longed to scream, but somehow the words wouldn't come. Why on earth had she allowed him to think otherwise for so long?

She had the long drive back to the *hacienda* to

dwell on her folly. She had no illusions about the nature of their marriage. It would be for life and there would be nothing platonic about it. Sebastian wanted children, he had told her so, and so did she, but up until now she hadn't allowed herself to think any further than the fact that she loved him. Now she was forced to concede that he believed her to be a sexually experienced woman; while in fact . . .

The hum of the powerful air-conditioning was the only sound to disturb the heavy silence of the car. Sebastian was driving the Mercedes himself, and his glance flicked from the road to her pale face, with dispassionate scrutiny.

'You are very pale. Do you not feel well?'

'A headache,' she managed to whisper, through a throat suddenly painfully constricted.

'That is the excuse of the married woman, not the bride,' Sebastian told her curtly. 'You are my wife, Jessica, and I will not have you reneging on our marriage now. There is something more than a headache troubling you—what is it?'

Was this the moment to tell him the truth? She cleared her throat hesitantly, wishing he would stop the car and take her in his arms. Somehow then it would be much easier to tell him that she was still a virgin.

'Stop playing games!' he warned her irately, swearing angrily as a cyclist suddenly wobbled into the centre of the road and he had to take evasive action. '*Por Dios*, my patience is almost at an end!' he muttered savagely. 'I can only thank God that I am spared the necessity of initiating a virgin. We were interrupted at a singularly inappropriate moment by my aunt and Pilar, and my need for the satisfaction their appearance denied me has been an aching hunger in my body ever since. But it is one which will be fully appeased tonight,' he added grimly, shocking her with his frankness.

'My payment for the privilege of bearing your name?' Jessica said tautly.

'Payment?' He frowned. 'What rubbish are you talking now? Your desire was as great as mine— you admitted it.'

And so she had, but that desire had been aroused by her love for him, and had been totally obliterated by her fear. How could she tell him the truth now?

'The others are a long way behind,' she murmured nervously at one point, glancing over her shoulder at the dust-covered road.

'They are indeed,' Sebastian agreed dryly, 'a full twenty-four hours behind. Tonight we shall be completely alone—my aunt's suggestion, and one I could not argue against. As it is, she points out to me that many of the family find it strange that we are returning to the *hacienda*.'

'I'm sure Pilar will acquaint them with the truth,' Jessica heard herself saying bitterly. 'That I trapped you into this marriage, just as you once thought I was trying to trap Jorge.'

'Pilar will say nothing,' Sebastian assured her coldly. 'And you are becoming hysterical—I cannot conceive why.'

No, Jessica raged inwardly, you wouldn't, would you? You're totally unfeeling and blind. If you weren't you'd know that I'm not ...

They turned into the drive leading to the house. Dusk had crept up on them as they drove, and the evening air was full of the scent of the flowers, the chirp of the crickets filling the silence.

As Sebastian had said, the house was completely and almost eerily empty. She felt his eyes on her back as she headed for the tower, freezing as he drawled mockingly,

'You are going the wrong way. From now on you will share my suite.'

His suite. His bed! Almost suffocating with the fear crawling through her body, Jessica allowed him to propel her towards another flight of stairs.

This was a part of the house she had not previously seen. A large but austere sitting room looked out on to a secluded, darkened courtyard. Lamps threw soft shadows across the room. It was decorated in soft mochas and creams; modern furniture that was entirely masculine. Expensive Italian units lined one wall, two dark brown velvet-covered settees placed opposite one another across an off-white expanse of carpet.

'The bedroom is through here.'

Jessica stared disbelievingly. Surely when he had talked about his desire he had not meant that he intended to satisfy it now?

She stared blankly at the door. It was barely seven o'clock, far too early to ... A hundred confused thoughts jumbled through her mind. She had been hoping to find a way of telling him the truth; had hoped that during the course of the evening his manner might soften a little ...

'I'm hungry,' she lied wildly, 'I ...'

'So am I,' Sebastian agreed obliquely, 'and I thought I had already warned you about playing games with me ... What are you trying to do?' he demanded brutally, 'drive me to the point where I'll commit rape? Does the thought of that turn you on, is that it?'

'No!' Jessica was totally revolted. 'I ...' 'I'm not ready' was what she wanted to say, but how could she? 'I'd like to shower and change, if you don't mind,' she managed with pathetic dignity. 'It's been a long day, and ...'

'Of course I don't mind,' he said smoothly. 'The shower is through there.'

He indicated a door across the width of the bedroom. As she craned her neck to see it, Jessica was acutely aware of his proximity, of the maleness he exuded and her own tremulous reaction to it.

'If you'll just excuse me for a second,' he drawled mockingly, 'there's something I have to do.'

At least he was affording her some brief respite, Jessica thought thankfully as she saw the sitting room door close behind her. He probably realised she would prefer to prepare for what was to come in private. The bedroom was as masculine as the sitting room, echoing its colours, with sliding patio doors into the courtyard. She flicked the light switch and instantly the room was bathed in soft light.

What about her clothes? she wondered anxiously. She could scarcely put back on her silk suit. She had just reached the sitting room door and opened it when Sebastian seemed to materialise out of nowhere.

'Going somewhere?' he asked sardonically.

'Er ... my clothes, I ...'

'You will find them in one of the cupboards.

The maids will have attended to it during the day.' He watched her lazily. 'Why so nervous? It cannot be the first time you have been in such a situation.'

'It's the first time I've been married, though,' Jessica managed tartly, almost instantly wishing she had been less aggressive when she saw the way his eyes darkened.

'Rafael has left us some chilled champagne. I shall go and pour some out, although I doubt that it will be consumed in the spirit he anticipates. He probably left it thinking that to drink it would held allay your maidenly qualms,' Sebastian explained succinctly when she glanced hesitantly at him.

At last he was gone, and Jessica searched feverishly through her clothes, finding clean underwear and a fresh dress. Luckily some of her clothes had arrived, and although there was nothing remotely bridal among them they brought a nostalgic touch of home.

The bathroom was luxuriously masculine; a deep dark red and cream, the bath enormous. After one brief glance at it, she opted for the shower, wishing fervently that the bathroom door had a lock, and then chiding herself for her lurid fears. She was behaving like a swooning Victorian heroine faced with her would-be ravisher. She loved Sebastian, she reminded herself.

But he didn't love her; and he didn't know that he would be her first lover.

The sting of the shower spray cooled her heated skin. Someone had placed her toiletries with Sebastian's and she used her perfumed shower gel to soap her body, enjoying the fragrance, but reminding herself that she mustn't linger. She was just about to turn on the water to wash off the soap when a deep voice murmured provocatively, 'You've missed a bit!'

Sebastian! She hadn't heard him enter the bathroom, and she turned quickly, reaching instinctively for a towel.

'Such modesty!' he mocked, twitching it away from her, 'and so unnecessary . . . mm?'

'Sebastian, please!' Her voice was curiously husky, a strange deep heat pervading her body, her head oddly light.

'There is no need to beg me, *querida*,' he drawled huskily, deliberately misunderstanding the nature of her plea. 'You are a very desirable woman, a little slender perhaps,' he mocked, and Jessica wondered if he was thinking of Pilar's lusher charms, 'but very tantalising for all that. I like your perfume,' he added softly, his finger moving along the ridge of her spine.

Panic clamoured inside her, her body tensing under the explorative caress, but Sebastian appeared not to notice. His fingers moved rhythmically over her skin, and as though he sensed that she was about to protest, he said softly, 'Like I said, you've missed a bit. What's the matter?' he asked, frowning as he sensed her tension.

'I . . . I'd like to get dressed,' she muttered huskily. 'As I said before, I'm hungry, and . . .'

'Like I said, so am I . . . I hope you're not getting any foolish ideas about reneging on our marriage. I want you, Jessica,' he told her coolly, 'and I want you now . . . Perhaps you're right,' he added softly, 'and now is not the time to play games in the shower. Later—er—when we have more leisure for playing. Right now, all I want is the scented warmth of your body in my arms, your heart beating against mine . . .'

'No!'

Jessica managed a husky protest, but it was lost, smothered as he lifted her out of the shower, careless of the dampness of her naked body against his clothes, carrying her effortlessly into the bedroom and depositing her on the bed.

'Beautiful,' he murmured with pleasure as his fingers drifted exploratively across her skin. 'So soft and pale.'

Jessica looked imploringly at the lamps revealing her body in its most intimate detail.

'You want us to make love in the darkness?' Strangely the idea seemed to displease him. 'Why?' he demanded. 'So that you can pretend I am someone else? Oh no, *querida*,' he told her tightly, 'I want you to know who it is who possesses you, and besides, your body is so beautiful I want to enjoy it with my eyes as well as my hands and lips. Just as I want you to enjoy mine,' he added seductively. 'A pity you had decided to shower before I could join you. I would have enjoyed undressing you.'

'I'm a woman, not a doll!' Jessica protested fiercely, terrified by the images his words were conjuring, the pulsating sensations radiating to every part of his body.

'Tonight you are my wife, and no matter what has gone before, it shall be as it has been with no other man, so that by morning you will remember only the touch of my hands, my body . . .'

And Jessica remembered the Moorish blood in his veins, the blatant sensuality that would be part of his legacy from that blood, and every muscle in her body constricted in terrified dread. He expected her to be a sexually experienced woman, instead of which . . .

She shivered, and he frowned, moving away from the bed, and returning with a glass of frothing liquid.

'Drink this,' he commanded. 'You are cold.'

The champagne bubbled in her throat, tickling her nose. She coughed, spilling some and feeling it splash down on her skin.

'*Dios*, but I want you,' Sebastian murmured throatily, then he bent his head, his tongue touching the spot where the champagne had fallen in the valley between her breasts. Tension coiled through her, a cramping sensation stirring in her stomach, weakness invading her muscles as his fingers gripped her hips and his mouth continued its subtle exploration of her breasts, first one and then the other—light, delicate caresses, the mere brush of his lips against her skin, tormenting her with the ache of unappeasement they left.

Her fear was forgotten. All she wanted was right here within reach. She groaned a half protest as Sebastian's lips continued their teasing assault, her fingers locking into his hair as she tried to silently convey her need for something more.

'You are too impatient,' he murmured against her skin. 'We have all night before us, your skin is as sweet and tender as a fresh peach, tempting to the tongue and firm to the touch.'

His hand left her hip to stroke wantonly across the soft tension of her stomach, his lips following a downward path.

'Sebastian . . .'

'How sweetly you say my name,' he told her huskily, 'and how much sweeter it would be to feel your lips against my skin. Surely, *querida*, I don't have to tell you that?'

He moved, and Jessica was instantly aware of his arousal, but a languid yielding sensation was spreading through her, driving out fear. Her fingers trembled over the buttons of his shirt, exploring the moistness of the skin beneath. His skin was warm, silk shielding hard muscle and bone, and merely to let her fingers drift over the smooth muscles of his back provoked a racing excitement that seemed to invade every nerve. His skin burned against her palms, his husky moan inciting her to press quivering lips against the smooth column of his throat, tasting the salty male scent of him.

'*Dios*, Jessica,' he protested hoarsely as her tongue delicately probed the curve of his throat, her hands clinging to his shoulders, the soft movements of her body inviting his touch. His hand cupped her jaw, imprisoning her as his mouth possessed hers with hot urgency, forcing her lips to part, tasting the moist inner sweetness. His hands moved urgently over her body, desire burning hotly in his eyes as he urged her to help him with his pants. He had none of the self-consciousness she possessed, his body golden and taut in the light from the lamps as he stood up briefly, watching her eyes move wonderingly.

'You look at me as though you have never seen

a man before, *querida*,' he told her softly. 'Such a look is a temptation to any man, and I am more than willing to be tempted.' He leaned over her, tanned fingers gently cupping first one breast and then the other as he bent his head, stroking the pulsating nipples lightly with his tongue, his mouth finally closing over the aching core, and waves of sensation beat through her as she gasped and trembled at the sensations he was arousing. A need to press wild, scattered kisses against his body seized her, his husky growl of pleasure reverberating along her spine.

His mouth left her breasts to stroke delicate kisses across her stomach, quivering with shock at the unaccustomed sensuality of his touch, but it seemed it wasn't enough simply for him to kiss her, she had to kiss him, and the feel of the tautly male flesh against her lips seemed only to increase the deep ache she could feel inside her. Then, as though he sensed her need and shared it, Sebastian parted her thighs, the heated masculinity of him unbearably arousing, as his tongue brushed softly over her lips, making her moan and cling desperately to his shoulders, mutely imploring him to cease tantalising her.

His mouth suddenly hardened on hers, his body taut with a need that communicated itself to every part of her. He moved, and suddenly, starkly, all her fear returned. There was pain and anger in his eyes, an anger which she had to blot out by closing hers, and weak tears seeped through as the sharp pain ended, taking with it her earlier euphoric pleasure.

'A virgin! You were a virgin,' Sebastian accused her. He was standing beside the bed wearing a dark silk robe, his hair tousled, and his expression bitter. 'Why didn't you tell me?'

'How could I?' Jessica muttered. 'I was going to when you started telling me how glad you were that I was a woman of experience ... Anyway, I don't see why you should complain,' she added acidly. 'It isn't many men who get to have two virgin brides ... Although, of course, in Manuela's case ...'

His jaw tightened in fury, all the muscles in his face tensing, and Jessica had the overwhelming suspicion that if she hadn't been a woman he would have hit her.

'You should be pleased,' she threw bitterly at him, refusing to give in to the tiny voice warning her not to go any further. 'I thought that was what all the Calvadores men expected in their brides—innocence, purity!'

'You should have told me,' he repeated icily.

'Why?' Tears weren't very far away, everything had gone disastrously wrong. In a corner of her heart Jessica had been hoping that somehow the discovery that she was a virgin might soften him towards her, but instead ... 'So that you could have been less ... excessive? Would it have made any difference? You would still have hurt me.'

It was a childish accusation, and her emotions were more bruised than her body, but his face closed up immediately, his expression grimly unreadable as he assured her curtly, 'In that case you may be sure that I will never ... hurt you again. I want no unwilling sacrifice in my bed,' he added cruelly.

'And there is always Pilar, isn't there?' Jessica flung at him. 'She's no shrinking virgin, to be shocked and distressed by your ... your demands!'

He laughed mirthlessly. 'My demands, as you call them, are no more than any sensual aroused male experiences. My mistake was in hoping to share them with you. Plainly you prefer to remain frigidly prudish. Then you may do so!'

CHAPTER EIGHT

IT had all gone disastrously wrong, Jessica thought numbly, listening to Tia Sofia while Lisa perched on her knee. The three of them were in the *sala* that Sofia had claimed as her own, drinking coffee and eating the cook's delicious almond biscuits.

Tia Sofia had been explaining to Jessica that they were expecting a visit from Sebastian's godfather and his daugher.

'*Querida*, are you not feeling well?' she broke off to ask Jessica with concern. 'You look pale—you have been indoors too much working on Sebastian's wretched designs, you must go out more.'

'Yes, you promised you would go for a walk with me,' Lisa reminded her reproachfully.

Assuring them both that she was fine, Jessica forced a smile to lips that felt as though they would crack from the constant effort of having to smile when it was the last thing she wanted to do. How could two people live as intimately as she and Sebastian did and yet remain so far apart? Initially she had expected him to suggest that they have separate bedrooms—he could hardly want to share his with her now, but to her dismay he did no such thing. Perhaps the terrible pride of the Calvadores would not allow him to admit that he did not desire his wife. Whatever the reason, she was forced to endure the humiliation, night after night, of knowing that he was lying merely inches away from her, but his attitude towards her was so cold and dismissive that they could have been separated by the Sierras.

And the strain was beginning to tell. More than once she thought she had glimpsed sympathy in Sofia's eyes, and she wondered if the older woman suspected the truth. She roused herself when Lisa repeated insistently that she had promised to go out with her.

The little girl was wearing another of her dainty dresses, and while they looked enchanting, Jessica wished she could see her in shorts and tee-shirts, getting grubby; living a more natural life.

'I wish Tio Sebastian was with us,' Lisa confided as they walked through the courtyard and past the swimming pool towards the outbuildings. 'When will he be back from Seville?'

'Tonight,' Jessica told her, trying not to admit to the sinking sensation she experienced whenever she thought of Sebastian. She had thought she had seen him angry before, but it was nothing compared with the icy hauteur with which she was now treated. How foolish she had been to think that her love was the key to his heart! He wanted neither her love nor her body.

'I'm going to show you my secret place,' Lisa told her importantly. 'No one knows about it but us . . . And Tio Sebastian.'

Lisa took her hand and led her towards the stable block. Her pony whinnied as they walked past, and they stopped to stroke his nose and feed him carrots from the bucket by the door.

'A long time ago this was where they made the wine,' Lisa told her importantly, opening a door into what Jessica had thought must be part of the converted garages, but which in fact she realised was a store place of some description. There was an old-fashioned wine press which she recognised from pictures, several large vats and some decaying barrels. 'It's down here, come on!'

Urged on by Lisa, she followed her to a cobwebby corner of the building, startled when Lisa motioned to another door. Jessica opened it, almost overbalancing on the steep flight of steps leading down from the door. As she glanced down the narrow, dark steps she felt a shuddering reluctance to descend them. She had always loathed the thought of being underground, but Lisa displayed no such qualms.

'It's fun, isn't it?' she demanded, leading the way with an agility that suggested she knew every step by heart. Jessica had to duck quickly to avoid the low roof as the steps suddenly turned and then levelled out.

They were in a rectangular room, illuminated by one single bare bulb suspended from a wire which ran the length of the ceiling. The ceiling itself was arched and composed of crumbling bricks. Moisture streamed off the walls, and the air felt cold and damp. Lisa, completely oblivious to Jessica's dislike of her treasured hidey-hole, beamed up at her with evident pleasure.

'No one ever comes down here now,' she told her. 'They used to store the barrels here a long time ago.'

She was going to have a word with Sebastian about allowing Lisa to wander so freely somewhere so potentially dangerous, Jessica decided when the top of the stairs was gained and they had switched off the light. It made her blood run cold just thinking what might happen to her alone down there. For one thing, the ceiling hadn't looked too safe; there had been deep fissures in some of the bricks.

They were on the way back to the house when Jorge suddenly caught up with them. He had been out riding and his hair was tousled from the exercise. He was an attractive boy, Jessica reflected, smiling warmly at him, but he was not Sebastian.

'Tio Jorge, Tio Jorge, put me down!' Lisa squealed, laughing as he swung her up in his arms and whirled her round and round.

'Not until you give me a kiss,' he threatened teasingly.

Obligingly she did so, while Jessica laughed. 'So that's the secret of your great charm, is it?' she mocked. 'Kisses by threats!'

'Be careful I don't do the same thing to you,' Jorge told her mock-threateningly, while Lisa announced earnestly, 'You can't kiss Jessica, Jorge, because she's married to Tio Sebastian!'

'Out of the mouths of babes,' Jorge drawled, sliding Jessica a sideways dancing glance. 'Not that I wouldn't like to try. My brother is a very lucky man.'

They were still laughing when they reached the courtyard, Lisa in the crook of one of Jorge's arms, while the other rested lightly on the back of Jessica's waist in a gesture more protective than provocative.

But the laughter drained out of Jessica's face

when she saw Sebastian's grimly angry face. He was sitting on the terrace with his aunt and Pilar, and all at once Jessica felt acutely aware of her untidy appearance, cobwebs no doubt clinging to her dress and hair, Jorge's arm on her waist.

'Jessica, had you forgotten Pilar was coming to see you this afternoon?'

Jessica shot a surprised glance at the Spanish woman's perfectly made up and bland face. As far as she knew they had made no such arrangements, nor was there any reason why they should do so. She didn't like Pilar and she knew the feeling was reciprocated. For one thing, she disliked the way Pilar treated Lisa, who was, after all, her sister's child.

To save any argument she apologised lightly, and was about to excuse herself to run upstairs and tidy up, when Pilar astounded her by saying, 'That is perfectly all right, Jessica. I quite understand. When one has an attractive man as an escort one tends to overlook engagements with one's woman friends.'

Sebastian looked thunderously angry, and Jessica bit her lip. Surely he didn't think she had deliberately ignored an engagement with Pilar? And Jorge—why was he looking at his brother in that evasive fashion, not explaining that they had simply met at the stables and walked back together?

Lisa, sensing the tension in the atmosphere, reached imploring for Sebastian's hand, her voice uncertain, her small face anxiously puckered. She was stretching on tiptoe and suddenly she over balanced, clutching the nearest thing to her for support, which happened to be Pilar's arm. The glass of *fino* Pilar was holding in her hand spilled down on to the cream silk dress she was wearing, and with a cry of rage she rounded on Lisa, taking her by the shoulders and shaking her furiously.

'This is too much, *querido*!' she complained to Sebastian. 'The child is uncontrollable and clumsy. I have told you before, she should be sent to a convent and taught how to conduct herself ... What may be suitable behaviour in an English household does not commend itself to our people. Perhaps you should explain that to your wife, for it is obvious that she has been encouraging Lisa to run wild. Clumsy girl!' she told Lisa, now pale and trembling, her dark brown eyes huge in her small face. 'When I was a child, I would have been whipped and sent to my room for the rest of the day for such unmannerly behaviour!'

Jessica longed to intervene. Her blood boiled in answering fury. How could Pilar terrorise Lisa so? It had been an accident; admittedly it was unfortunate that the sherry should have been spilled, but Jessica doubted that the cream silk was the only dress in Pilar's wardrobe, or that she couldn't replace it quite easily.

'Perhaps you are right, *querida*,' she heard Sebastian saying evenly. 'Lisa, you will apologise to your aunt, and then I think you will go to your room ...'

'It is probably more Jessica's fault than Lisa's,' Pilar added maliciously. 'Have you seen how grubby the child is? She is probably over-excited.'

'My wife does seem to have that effect on some

people,' Sebastian agreed coldly. 'Lisa,' he commanded, looking at the little girl, 'I have told you once to go to your room, I will not do so again!'

Jessica saw his aunt check a response, her expression unhappy, and all her own indignation boiled over.

'It was an accident,' she interrupted hotly. 'Poor Lisa is no more to blame than ... anyone else. Sebastian, I ...'

'Be careful, Jessica,' Pilar mocked. 'Sebastian does not like to have his decisions queried, do you, *querido*?'

Jessica ignored her. 'Come, Lisa, I'll take you upstairs,' she said softly, hating the hurt pain in the little girl's eyes. She had just seen her god topple from his plinth, Jessica suspected, still unable to understand why Sebastian had spoken so harshly.

Dinner was always a formal occasion in the Calvadores household, but it had never been as silently tense as it was tonight, Jessica thought to herself as she refused any caramel pudding in favour of a cup of coffee.

'Señor Alvarez and Luisa arrive tomorrow, will you collect them from the airport?'

'I have some work to complete on the designs,' Sebastian said curtly. He had hardly spoken to any of them during the meal, and Jessica thought she might be wrong, but there was a controlled tension about him she had never noticed before. Was it because of their marriage? Was he, like her, wishing it had never taken place?

'I could go,' Jorge offered. 'I could take Jessica and Lisa with me.'

'I think not,' Sebastian cut in coldly. 'The car will be cramped with five of you, and besides, it is time that Lisa learned that good manners are something that cannot be discarded simply at whim. She will remain indoors tomorrow as a reminder.'

'Does that apply to me too?' Jessica demanded, temper flags flying in her cheeks. 'Am I to be "sent to my room", for forgetting Pilar's invitation?'

Sebastian's mouth compressed into a thin hard line. 'Lisa is at an age where her nature can still be moulded and formed. Regrettably, you are not. Now, if you will excuse me, I have work to do.'

'Phew!' Jorge grimaced when he had gone. 'He has a black monkey riding on his back tonight, hasn't he? Have you two had a quarrel?'

Quarrel! Jessica suppressed hysterical laughter. To have a quarrel they would need to talk, to share an emotion. They weren't close enough to quarrel.

'Sebastian is tired,' Tia Sofia palliated. 'He has been working too hard. I have warned him before . . .'

'I didn't know Pilar intended to visit me,' Jessica explained to his aunt, not wanting her too to think she had been remiss.

'Pilar tends to be a little possessive towards Sebastian,' Sofia said gently, 'and sometimes that prompts her into actions of impulse. I'm sure she did not mean to cause any friction between you.'

Jessica said nothing. She was pretty sure that was exactly what Pilar had wanted to do, but she had no intention to saying so to the others.

'Has Sebastian said anything to you about Barbara?' Jorge asked her half an hour later as they wandered through the courtyard.

'Nothing,' Jessica told him, without adding that it was hardly likely that he would do so.

'He is annoyed with me, I am afraid, but I cannot marry a girl I do not love.'

It was a sentiment Jessica wholly appreciated. 'Of course not,' she agreed sympathetically.

The courtyard was illuminated by a full moon, bathing everything in soft silver light. The air was warm, almost too warm, and curiously still.

'We could be in for a storm,' Jorge commented as they headed back to the house. 'We need rain badly. It has been a very dry spring.' His sleeve brushed against Jessica's bare arm and he stopped her suddenly, his hand on her shoulder as he turned her towards him.

'You are so very different from your cousin,' he said softly. 'She is a taker from others, while you are a giver, but be careful you don't give my brother too much. He has a devil riding him that cannot be exorcised. He has been this way since Manuela died.'

What was he trying to tell her? That Sebastian still loved Manuela? Tears stung her eyes and she lowered her head, taking momentary comfort from Jorge's presence before turning to return to the house.

As always, she felt a reluctance to go upstairs. Sebastian was never there. He always worked late—avoiding the awful moment when he must join her, Jessica thought bitterly. If she had hoped that somehow the fact of her virginity might incline him towards her she had been bitterly disappointed. And the mutual desire he had spoken of so freely before they were married might never have existed. Jessica didn't know what was responsible for the change in him—but she hated the long, empty nights when she lay sleepless at his side, knowing she had only to stretch out her hand to touch him, and knowing it was the one thing she must never do. And humiliatingly she still wanted to touch him; it was there like an alien growth inside her, this need to touch and know. She couldn't forget his final cruel words to her on the night of their wedding, and there was still an unappeased ache within her that throbbed like an exposed nerve whenever she thought about how it had felt to be in his arms.

She opened the bedroom door, stiffening with shock as she saw the moonlit figure by the patio door.

'So you have returned.' Sebastian's voice was flat and unemotional. 'I thought after what I just witnessed that you might have decided to spend the night with my brother.'

For a moment Jessica stared uncomprehendingly at him, and then enlightenment dawned.

'Jorge and I were simply talking,' she protested, silenced by the harsh sound of his laughter.

'The way you had been simply talking this afternoon, I suppose,' he said savagely.

It was useless to tell him that she had simply met Jorge on the way back from her outing with Lisa, but at the thought of the little girl, she remembered the tear-stained face and trembling mouth when she had gone in to say goodnight to her, and read her the story they were both enjoying.

'You were very unfair to Lisa this afternoon,' she told him angrily, able to defend his daughter if she couldn't defend herself. 'It was an unfortunate accident, but she was in no way to blame. Pilar always contrives to upset her. She adores you, Sebastian, and you were viciously cruel to her. I can't understand why you turned on her like that.'

'You can't? Perhaps it's because a wounded animal does claw at other things in its agony; perhaps it's because I'm going out of my mind with frustration,' he told her bluntly. 'When I married you it was not with the intention that our marriage should be platonic.'

'I should have told you the truth,' Jessica admitted huskily. 'I wanted to, but . . .'

'But you preferred to let me find out the hard way—for us both—and then you turn to my brother for solace. Well, you may not find solace in my arms, Jessica,' he told her brutally, 'but I'm no saint to burn in the fires of hell when the means of quenching them is at hand. You were prepared to give yourself to my brother, now you can give yourself to me!'

Her panicky protest was lost against his mouth, storming her defences, sending waves of heat pulsating through her body. Instantly everything was forgotten but the wild clamouring in her blood, the need for his possession which had been aching inside her ever since their wedding night, although never fully acknowledged.

'I want you,' Sebastian muttered thickly against her mouth, 'and when I take you, you will think only of me, not my brother, not anyone but me. It will be my name you cry out in the fiery midst of passion; my body that gives yours the ultimate sweet pleasure.'

A shaft of moonlight illuminated his face, drawn and shadowed, so that Jessica could almost deceive herself that it was pain she saw in his eyes. Was he thinking of Manuela when he spoke to her? A sharp stabbing pain shot through her, her small moan of protest igniting a ferocity within him that shocked and excited as he stripped her swiftly, his face a mask of concentration, his hands only stilling when he had removed everything but her minute briefs.

The knowledge that he wanted her trembled though her on an exultant wave, and slowly she reached towards him, unfastening the buttons of his shirt, sliding her hands across the breadth of his chest and feeling it lift and tense with the sudden urgency of his breathing. Her marauding fingers were trapped and held against his heart as it pounded into her palm, and a curious sensation of timelessness gripped her.

This time she felt no shyness at the sight of his naked body, rather a desire to touch and know it, but his smothered groan as her fingertips stroked lightly against his thigh warned her of the intensity of his need. His hands cupped her breasts, his mouth following the line of her throat and shoulders, before returning to fasten hungrily on hers. His body burned and trembled against her, sweat beading his forehead and dampening his skin.

On a swiftly rising spiral of excitement Jessica explored the maleness of his body, feeling the increasing urgency within him; the blind hunger that made him shudder under her touch, and she knew beyond any doubt that this time nothing would appease the ache inside her but the hard, demanding pressure she could feel building up inside him.

She wanted his possession of her body with a need that went beyond anything she had ever experienced. Her hips writhed and arched, and Sebastian groaned against her throat, holding her, shaping her until she was formless and malleable, her only purpose in life to fulfil the explosive ache that possessed her every conscious thought and action.

'Sebastian . . .' She moaned his name under his caressing hands, trying to communicate her need, but instead of fulfilling her, he stilled. She opened desire-drugged eyes and stared at him uncomprehendingly, a tiny protest leaving her lips.

'Sebastian, please!' Her fingers curled into the smooth muscles of his back, her mind still shying away from actually telling him how much she needed him, while her body ached wantonly for her to do so, no matter what the cost.

'You want me.'

It was a statement rather than a question, but something forced her to respond to it, her nervous, husky, 'Very much,' making his eyes darken until they were almost black, his breathing suddenly altered and uneven. '*Dios*, Jessica,' he told her rawly, 'I want you, even though I know . . .'

She didn't want him to say more, to spoil what was between them with any words that might make her face up to the truth. Now lying in his arms, the full weight of his body pressed against hers, she could almost convince herself that he could love her, but if he spoke, if he said that word 'want' again when she wanted to hear him say 'love', it would burst her protective bubble, and that was something she didn't want. So in desperation she pressed her finger to his lips and then clasped her hands behind his neck drawing him down towards her, running her tongue softly over his lips, tracing the firm outline of them, until, suddenly, he muttered a husky protest, capturing her face with his hands and holding it still while his mouth moved hungrily over hers and the heated pressure of his thighs ignited a heat that spread swiftly through her body until it welcomed his shuddering thrust, rejoicing in the bittersweet mingling of pain and pleasure, knowing with some prescient knowledge that this time he was tempering his need so that she could share fully the pleasure of their entwined bodies.

And then all thought was superseded as swiftly urgent pleasure contracted through her body and she was free-soaring into realms of delight she had never dreamed existed.

When she woke up she was alone; there was a dent in the pillow where Sebastian's head had lain, but no other traces of his presence. Jessica swung her legs out of the bed, surprised to discover how lethargic and weak she felt. She steadied herself as the room spun round, and faintness overwhelmed her. Just for a moment she wished Sebastian was there, to take her in his arms, and kiss her with the tenderness a man might reserve for the woman he had just made wholly his, if he loved her, but then she banished the thought. Perhaps last night would lead to other improvements in their marriage. Perhaps his desire for her might lead Sebastian to treat her with tenderness and affection.

She had forgotten that he had said he was going to Seville and was disappointed to get downstairs and find him gone. Jorge was at the breakfast table, trying to cheer up a tearful Lisa.

Jessica had started going with Tia Sofia when she discussed the day's menus and work plans with the staff. The *hacienda* was enormous, with so many valuable antiques and works of art that cleaning it had to be organised with almost military precision. Many of the staff had inherited their jobs from their mothers and fathers, and all were devoted to the family. Jessica had found that they treated her with respect and affection, and when she murmured to Sofia that she was sure she would never be able to cope as admirably as she did, the older woman had laughed.

'You will,' she had told her, 'and before very long as well. You have a natural flair with people.'

If she did, it didn't extend to include her husband, Jessica thought ruefully.

Lisa was so unhappy that Jessica spent a large part of the morning with her. Her part of the designing work was now almost complete until Sebastian came to a final decision. She had received a delighted letter from her aunt and uncle, full of exclamations and wishes that they had been able to attend her wedding.

'Isabel gets married in three months' time,' her aunt had written, 'and of course you must be there. She was going to ask you to be bridesmaid, but now it will have to be matron of honour. John's parents are holding the reception at their house—there's to be a marquee in the garden, and John's mother is a splendid organiser, so I won't have anything to worry about other than finding an outfit.'

As she folded the letter Jessica sighed. Would Isabel be any happier than she was? She certainly hoped so.

In an effort to try and cheer Lisa up, she taught her to play Snap with an old pack of cards she had found, and although she played dutifully, her eyes kept straying to the door. How could Sebastian have been so cruel to her? Jessica fumed. His own child, even if he did refuse to acknowledge her. This cruel streak in a man who was so otherwise so strong was a weakness that caused her concern. His pride she could understand and even forgive, but his refusal to tell Lisa her true parentage was something that worried her.

'Will Tio Sebastian really send me away to a convent?' Lisa asked her at one point, her chin wobbling slightly.

'I'm sure he won't,' Jessica told her, trying to comfort her.

'But when you have babies, he won't want me,' Lisa appalled her by confiding. 'Pilar told me so.'

'Of course we'll still want you,' Jessica assured her, inwardly wondering how Pilar could be so deliberately malicious. 'What shall we do this afternoon?' she asked her, trying to redirect her thoughts. But Lisa refused to respond.

Jorge returned with the visitors from South America just after lunch. Señor Alvarez, Sebastian's godfather, turned out to be a genial, plump South American, who kissed both Jessica and Sofia enthusiastically, his eyes twinkling as he told Sofia that she didn't look a day older.

'Then you must need new glasses,' Sebastian's aunt told him practically, 'for it is over twenty years since we last met.'

'I remember it as though it were yesterday,' he assured her. 'You were then a bride of six months, and how I envied my cousin! Just as I'm sure many men must envy Sebastian,' he added gallantly, turning to Jessica. 'Jorge tells me that he has to work but that he will return in time for dinner. You must not let him work so hard—all work and no play, don't you English have a saying about that?'

'Sebastian has a black monkey on his back at the moment,' Jorge interrupted cheerfully. 'Poor Lisa felt the weight of his temper yesterday, and all because of that cat Pilar Sanchez.'

'Ah, Pilar!' Señor Alvarez grimaced. 'A very feline woman, is that one. I shall have to take care to guard my little Luisa from her claws!'

He drew his daughter forward to be introduced, and Jessica noticed the look in Jorge's eyes as they rested on her. Small and dainty, her glossy black hair was drawn back off her face, her huge pansy-brown eyes were nervous and hesitant as they were introduced. She couldn't be more than eighteen, Jessica reflected, but already she had the ripeness, the innocent sensuality of Latin women.

At Jorge's suggestion she allowed herself to be

detached from the others to explore the courtyards. The *hacienda* was so different from the style of architecture she was accustomed to that she was eager to explore.

'Your daughter is extremely lovely,' Jessica commented warmly when they had gone.

'She is a crimson velvet rose,' her father agreed poetically, 'but many men prefer the beauty of the golden rose that grows best in the cooler climes of the north.'

Señor Alvarez had come to Spain on business as well as pleasure, and when he discovered that Jessica had been helping Sebastian with his new designs he started to talk to her with great enthusiasm and interest about wool and South America. Jessica found it all fascinating; he was an entertaining companion; scholarly, and yet worldly enough to add a little salt to his speech, and like all Latins, he was an expert at turning a neat compliment. Sebastian had never complimented her, Jessica realised with a shock. He had never flirted with her either. The tiny cold lump of unhappiness she had felt on waking and discovering that he had gone grew and refused to be banished.

Sebastian eventually returned to the *hacienda* just before dinner. Pilar had been invited to join this celebratory meal, mainly because she knew the Alvarez family well, and as she was a widow, it was perfectly permissible for her to join a family party without a male escort.

She arrived just as they were sipping sherry in the *sala*, her black silk evening dress a perfect foil for her dark beauty and curvaceous figure. In comparison, Jessica felt pale and insignificant in her softly draped cream chiffon suit with its camisole top and loose jacket, even though she had loved it when she tried it on in the shop.

Luisa, as befitted a young girl, was wearing a plain dress in white, and pretty though it was, Jessica didn't think it did the younger girl's complexion justice.

Sebastian had been late joining them and had come into the room only minutes before Pilar, who, the moment she saw him, made a beeline for him, linking her arm with his in a very proprietorial manner, scarlet fingernails like drops of blood against the darkness of his jacket, as she laughed and joked with Señor Alvarez.

'Have you been in to see Lisa?' Jessica managed to ask Sebastian quietly before they went in to dinner. 'She's been moping all day because you were so cross with her.'

She didn't think anyone else had heard her until Pilar turned round suddenly, her eyes raking Jessica's face coldly, her voice falsely sweet as she said smoothly,

'I must go up and see her too before I go. Lisa is suddenly displaying a very naughty strain,' she added for Señor Alvarez' benefit. 'I'm afraid I had to be quite cross with her yesterday.'

Sebastian hadn't answered her question, and Jessica was afraid to ask it again. All her hopes that somehow last night might have had a softening effect on his attitude to her had been destroyed the moment he walked into the *sala*, his face grimly blank as he sought her out and with meticulous politeness enquired about her day. His very politeness seemed to hold her deliberately at a distance as though he wanted to warn her not to try to come too close. Had his love for Manuela been such that he could never love anyone else? Had her death frozen his emotions, making it impossible for him to feel anything other than desire for another woman?

Jessica sighed, reflecting that the evening ahead wasn't likely to be an easy one. Already she could see that Jorge was being more than simply politely attentive to Luisa and that she was responding with glowing eyes and happy smiles. Sebastian hadn't noticed yet, but when he did . . .

Jorge hadn't been forgiven for refusing to marry Barbara, although privately Jessica thought it was very wrong of Sebastian to attempt to dictate to his brother whom he should marry. But of course that was the Spanish way.

The night was hot and stuffy, thunder growling in the distance. Halfway through the meal Jessica was attacked by a wave of nausea and dizziness, which, fortunately, she managed to fight off. She didn't believe anyone had noticed, until she realised that Pilar was watching her with narrowed, assessing eyes. Trying to dislodge the cold feeling of disquiet she always felt when the other woman watched her, Jessica discreetly refrained from eating much more. Doubtless it was the overpowering heat and threatening storm that was making her feel so odd, and at least Sebastian seemed more relaxed, as he chatted to his godfather. She heard him mention her name and listened, wondering what was being said.

'Your husband has just been praising your ability as a designer,' Señor Alvarez told her, with a smile. 'He tells me that your ideas are nothing short of inspired.'

Again Jessica was conscious of Pilar's malevolent regard, but she tried to ignore it. Sebastian praising her! A tiny thrill of pleasure lightened the ice packed round her heart. Perhaps after all there might be some future for them; some basis on which they could build the foundations of a relationship.

CHAPTER NINE

'TIA SOFIA, have you seen Lisa?' Jessica had been looking for the little girl for half an hour, but no one had seen her since lunchtime. She glanced out of the window at the black sky and pounding rain. Surely Lisa wouldn't have ventured outside? The rain fell in sheets rather than drops, bouncing on the hard dry earth, and on the radio there had been flood warnings.

Sebastian had been concerned for the vines, although he explained that fortunately they were not at a stage in their development when too much damage would be done. The poorer growers might suffer some losses, Jorge had told Jessica later, but Sebastian, together with other wealthy landlords, had formed an association that could help the small growers through difficult patches.

'He takes his responsibilities as head of our family very seriously,' Jorge explained to her. 'Too seriously, I sometimes think, perhaps because he was so young when he had to take over from our father.'

And he had had to take over alone, Jessica reflected, without Manuela at his side.

'I'm getting worried about Lisa,' she confided in Sofia with a frown when no one could remember seeing the little girl. 'Where can she be?'

'She has been very upset recently,' Sofia

agreed, echoing Jessica's concern. 'I told Sebastian he had been too harsh with her, but he seems to have devils of his own to fight at the moment.'

'I think I'll go upstairs and check again that she isn't in her room—she might just have slipped out,' Jessica commented.

'If you don't find her, we'll organise a search. Children get odd ideas into their head when they're upset—even the most sensible of them.'

Lisa wasn't in her room, but Jessica bumped into the girl Maria, who looked after her, as she came out. She looked worried and upset.

'Have you seen Lisa?' Jessica asked her. The girl shook her head.

'Not since morning,' she told Jessica. 'She was very upset, the little one. Last night . . .' she bit her lip, flushing and hesitating.

'Yes, go on,' Jessica urged her. 'Last night . . .?'

'Well, it is just that Señora Sanchez came up to see her. I had gone downstairs to get her some hot milk to help her sleep, and when I came back I could hear their voices. Señora Sanchez was very, very angry. I could hear her shouting, but I didn't go in. When she came out she didn't see me, and I went into the room and found Lisa crying. The Señora had told her that she was to be punished for being naughty and that the Conde was to send her away—to a school where they would be very strict with her—and that she would never be allowed to come back.'

Jessica was appalled and looked it. How could Pilar be so heartless, and why had Sebastian not confided his plans to *her*? Of course Pilar was Lisa's aunt, but surely he might have consulted her before deciding to send Lisa away to school?

She had been intending to suggest that there might be a good school in Seville she could attend, and that during the week they could live in the house there to be with her. How could he treat his daughter so unkindly?

'I tried to comfort her,' Maria went on to say, 'but it was many hours before she went to sleep.'

'You should have come and told me,' Jessica said remorsefully, hating to think of Lisa lying awake and crying while they were dining downstairs unaware of her misery. 'Did she say anything this morning?' probed.

Maria shook her head. 'Not a word. She was very subdued and quiet, but she said nothing.'

Feeling more apprehensive than she wanted to admit, Jessica hurried back downstairs to give Tia Sofia the news.

She too looked grave when Jessica had finished. 'You say Pilar told her that Sebastian was to send her to school? I cannot believe he would come to such a decision without telling us first. Do you think she could have exaggerated?'

It was a thought, but Jessica felt that not even Pilar would have dared to tell such a barefaced and hurtful lie without some justification.

Jorge was summoned and told of their fears, and Señor Alvarez, who had accompanied him, was quick to suggest that they each take portions of the house to search.

'Sebastian must be told,' he added firmly.

'I'll telephone him,' Jorge agreed. 'Unless, of course . . .' he glanced at Jessica, but she shook her head. She didn't trust herself to speak logically to Sebastian at the moment; she was too

concerned about Lisa. She thought of the little
girl's misery and was overwhelmed by a sensation
of nauseous sickness. She had felt slightly unwell
when she first woke up and had put it down to
the richness of the food at dinner last night and
the fact that her system had still not grown
accustomed to eating so late.

'You are not well?' Señor Alvarez had seen her
pale face and hurried to her side.

'It's nothing,' she assured him. 'I'm fine now.'
She saw the glance he and Sofia exchanged and
was puzzled by it, until she murmured discreetly
to her,

'I have noticed on a few occasions recently that
you have not seemed well. Could it be . . .?'

It was a few minutes before Jessica realised
what she meant. Could she be carrying
Sebastian's child? Surely it was too soon to know,
and besides, there had only been those two
occasions . . .

One of which would have been more than
enough, she reminded herself grimly, panic
clawing through her at the implications. She
wasn't ready yet for the responsibility of a child.
Her relationship with Sebastian was too fraught
with difficulties; they had no right to bring a
child into such an insecure marriage. Children
should be wanted, surrounded with love and care.

She was letting her imagination run away with
her, she decided later, as she listened to Señor
Alvarez speaking quickly to Sebastian. She
probably wasn't pregnant at all.

'Sebastian is returning immediately,' he told
them. 'Meanwhile we must do all we can to find
her.'

Señor Alvarez quickly took command, much to Jessica's relief. They were each given different sections of the house to seach, apart from Luisa, who elected to help Jorge with his.

Jessica walked with them to the top of the stairs, thinking it was a pity that if Sebastian had to arrange a marriage for his brother he didn't do so with pretty little Luisa, who plainly was quite ready to fall in love with him, just as he was with her.

She was halfway through her own part of the *hacienda* when suddenly a thought struck her. She hurried downstairs and out into the courtyard, ignoring the heavy rain as she dashed across to the stables. She had hoped to find Enrico, who was in charge of the horses there, but he had obviously taken shelter somewhere, because the place was deserted. The first thing Jessica noticed as she approached the building Lisa had shown her was that the roof was dipping badly under a weight of water. Once inside she realised that it was also leaking because the floor was damp, but she didn't waste any time worrying about the dampness, hurrying instead across to the cellar door, wrenching it open and anxiously calling Lisa's name. The light was on, and she thought she heard a faint reply, when suddenly almost overhead there was a terrific clap of thunder. She eyed the steps uncertainly. Moisture trickled down the walls, the light was dull and pale, and she felt an increasing aversion to go down, but Lisa might be down there, hurt or frightened. She hesitated, wondering whether to dash back to the house, acknowledging that she should have gone to Señor Alvarez in the first place and told him of her fears. She was just about to go when she heard a sound. Straining her ears, she caught it again. Lisa! She was down there!

'Don't worry, Lisa,' she called out, 'I'm coming down!'

She had almost reached the bottom when she heard a sound, a dull heavy rumbling which she tried to tell herself was thunder, but which instinct told her was something much worse. The only sound she had ever heard to resemble it was avalanches witnessed on television, and there was certainly no snow on the *hacienda*. There was water, though, she reflected nervously, remembering the dilapidated roof, bowing under the weight of water. If that roof collapsed! She daren't allow herself to think about it. Terror clawed painfully at her stomach and she crossed her hands protectively over it, knowing in a blinding moment of realisation that she *did* want Sebastian's child.

Somehow the thought that she might already have conceived it made her feel all the more protective towards Lisa. Half running, half stumbling, she hurried down the steep steps, searching the cavern at the bottom with frantic intensity, until she saw the little girl at the farthest end, her face tear-stained.

'Oh, Lisa!'

'Jessica, I can't get up,' Lisa cried plaintively. 'I fell and hurt my ankle. I thought I was going to be here for ever!'

'Hush, darling, it's all right,' Jessica comforted her, hurrying over and crouching on the floor beside her. 'Let me look,' she said gently, running her fingers over the little girl's leg and ankle-bone. She thought it was more sprained than broken, but she couldn't let Lisa risk putting any weight on it. She would have to carry her out.

'Put your arms round my neck,' she instructed, 'and hold on tight. It might hurt a little bit, but just think of how quickly we're going to be back in the house. You gave us all a nasty fright, you know,' she went on, talking quietly as she tried to make Lisa as comfortable as she could. 'Tio Sebastian is coming back from Seville to help us look for you.'

'But you found me,' Lisa protested drowsily, gasping as Jessica tried to lift her. Dear God, what if she had banged her head when she fell? She could have concussion—anything! Should she leave her and go and get help?

'Don't let Tio send me to school, will you?' Lisa begged tearfully.

'Is that why you came down here, so you wouldn't have to go to school?'

Lisa shook her head. 'I just wanted to think,' she said simply, and they both winced as they heard a loud rumbling overhead.

'Only thunder,' Jessica said firmly. She glanced upwards and stared in horror at the crack appearing in the arched ceiling. Dirt and rubble trickled down, spattering on to the floor, the light bulb swinging wildly before the cavern was suddenly plunged into darkness. With the light gone Jessica's ears became attuned to sounds she had not heard before—the steady trickling of moisture on the walls, the ominous rumblings from above them, and the slowly increasing dribble of debris through the now invisible crack in the ceiling.

She couldn't possibly leave Lisa now, Jessica acknowledged. In fact neither of them could stay where they were for a moment longer than they had to.

'We've got to move,' she told the little girl, relieved when Lisa answered in a matter-of-fact if somewhat breathless voice,

'Yes, otherwise the roof might fall in on us, mightn't it?'

'Well, just hold on tight,' Jessica cautioned her.

Surely the best thing to do would be to feel her way along the wall. That way they were more likely to avoid any cave-in. It was a painfully laborious task inching her way along the wall, trying her best not to jar Lisa's ankle. She had no idea how far they had gone when they both heard the sudden crack above, and it was only blind instinct that sent her stumbling for the stairs, her head bent over Lisa's as they were showered with debris and the water that cascaded through the hole in the ceiling.

She could have cried with relief when she felt the first step; she had been terrified that they were going to be trapped by the falling ceiling. Her body was trembling with tiredness and relief when they finally reached the top stair. She fumbled for the catch and pushed, but the door refused to open. She tried again, forcing her whole weight behind it, and still it refused to move.

'Something must have blocked it,' Lisa murmured apprehensively. 'What are we going to do?'

'We're going to sit here and wait for someone to come and unblock it,' Jessica told her, trying to appear calm.

'But no one knows we're here.'

It was all too dreadfully true. What could she say? Taking a deep breath, Jessica lied, 'Oh yes, they do—I told Jorge I thought you might be here, but I didn't say anything before, because I didn't think you'd want me to tell anyone else about your secret place.'

'Now four of us know,' Lisa replied drowsily. 'You, me, Tio Sebastian and Tio Jorge.'

Yes, Sebastian knew, but did he care enough about either of them to think of looking here? Eventually someone was bound to notice that the roof had caved in, but they might not realise that they had been trapped in the cellar.

Dreadful pictures flashed through her mind, stories of walled-up nuns and petrified skeletons tormenting her until she wanted to scream and beat on the door until it gave way, but if she did that it would only upset Lisa. She would perhaps never know whether she had been carrying Sebastian's child, and he would have lost another bride, although this time ... She sighed and shivered as the cold sliced through to her bones.

Lisa's teeth were chattering; the little girl was only wearing a flimsy dress and Jessica pulled off her own knitted jacket, draping it round her shoulders and pulling her into the warmth of her own body.

Time dragged by. Jessica wasn't wearing a watch, and the only sounds to break the silence were their own voices and the ominous cracking sounds as more of the ceiling gave way.

Lisa started to cry. 'We'll be trapped in here for ever,' she sobbed. 'We'll never get out!'

'Of course we will. Look, I'll tell you a story, shall I?'

She did her best, inventing impossible characters and situations, but she only had a tiny portion of Lisa's concentration.

'Stop!' she insisted at one point. 'Jessica, I thought I heard something.'

Her heartbeat almost drowning out her ability to say anything else, Jessica listened. There were sounds ... faint, but clearly discernible from those of the falling ceiling.

'We must shout,' Lisa urged, 'so that they know we're here.'

'No, we'll tap on the door instead,' Jessica told her, terrified that if they shouted the reverberations might be enough to bring down what was left of the ceiling.

She tapped, and there was no response, and no matter how much she strained her ears she could hear nothing from the other side of the door. Perhaps they had simply imagined those sounds after all, perhaps there wasn't anyone there—or even worse, perhaps someone had been and gone.

'We must keep tapping,' she told Lisa doggedly, not wanting the little girl to lose heart.

Her wrist was aching with the effort of supporting Lisa and trying to tap on the door at the same time, when at last she heard a faint but unmistakable response. Just to be sure she tapped again—Morse code learned when she was a girl and only dimly remembered, the same definite pattern of sounds coming back to her.

Tears of relief poured down her face. Her chest

felt tight with pain, and she could scarcely think for relief.

The sounds outside the door became louder and took on definite patterns; at the same time more of the roof came crashing down, bricks and rubble falling sharply on to the steps. It was a race between life and death, Jessica thought, shivering at the knowledge, and they were the prize.

A piece of brick fell on her foot, but she scarcely felt any pain. She was so cold her body was practically numb.

'How long to you think it will be?' Lisa asked huskily. 'I'm so cold, Jessica!'

'Not long now,' she comforted her. There was a splintering sound above them, followed by a high-pitched whine. In the darkness Jessica could see nothing, but she could feel a faint dust settling on her face. They must be cutting through the door. A tiny glimmer of light appeared, followed by a small hole.

'Jessica?' It was Sebastian's voice, crisp and sharp. 'Jessica, where are you?'

'We're here,' she told him tiredly, hugging Lisa. 'At the top of the steps.'

'Listen carefully, then. The roof has collapsed and the door is jammed. We're going to cut the top half away, but whatever you do, don't move from where you are. We think there's been some subsidence underneath and the shift of your weight might cause the steps to collapse.'

'Lisa's hurt her ankle,' she told him, 'but I think it's only sprained.'

There were sounds of further activity beyond the door. The thin beam of light grew and at last she could see Lisa's face. She could also see how precarious their position was. Where the cellar had been there was simply a mound of rubble, and she shuddered to think of their fate had they been trapped beneath it. Several of the lower steps were already cracked, and even as she watched the cracks deepened and spread. At last the buzzing of the saw ceased, and light flooded their prison. She looked up, joy and love flooding her eyes as she saw Sebastian looking down at them.

'Take Lisa first,' she told him, lifting the little girl. His face was smudged with dirt, his hair ruffled and untidy, a curiously bleak expression in his eyes.

'Sebastian, hurry, the whole thing's going to go at any minute!' she heard Jorge call behind him, and she realised that Sebastian was alone in the crumbling shell of the building.

She also realised that she couldn't scramble over the half door without some help and that she would have to stay here alone while he carried Lisa to safety. He seemed to hesitate as though he guessed her fear, but she forced a smile, and lifted Lisa towards him.

His arms closed round her and he turned. Watching his back disappear into the darkness was the most terrifying and lonely feeling Jessica had ever experienced. When he disappeared she wanted to claw and tear at the wood in panic, but no matter how much she stretched she couldn't get over the wooden barrier. Behind her she heard a dull crack, and gasped in horror as half the steps suddenly disappeared, leaving her clinging to the door.

'Jessica, Jessica, it's all right, I've got you!' Strong arms clamped round her body, lifting her upwards, as she clung unashamedly to their warm strength.

It was only as he lifted her over the door that Jessica realised the appalling risks Sebastian had run. The building was completely demolished, a yawning chasm gaped beneath them. As Sebastian carried her to safety she heard a dull rumble, and glanced over his shoulder just in time to see the ground sliding away, taking the remnants of the building with it.

'It's the rain,' Jorge muttered as Sebastian reached him. Señor Alvarez was with him, holding Lisa, and both men were soaked to the skin, their faces anxious and drawn. Jessica hadn't even realised it was still raining until that moment, and she felt she had never enjoyed anything quite as much as the rain against her skin, and the cold breeze blowing down from the Sierras. 'It eroded away the ground beneath and the sheer weight of the building caused it to collapse.'

'If Sebastian hadn't remembered Lisa's "secret place" we might never have found you,' Señor Alvarez said gravely as they hurried towards the house. 'It is a blessing that he reached you in time.'

It was indeed, Jessica reflected numbly, shivering with the cold that seemed to reach into her bones, despite the warmth of Sebastian's arms.

In the house Tia Sofia was waiting, fear etched deeply into her face until she saw the two burdens Sebastian and Jorge were carrying.

'Lisa has hurt her ankle,' Jorge told her quickly. 'Doctor . . .'

'I shall telephone him now . . . but first we must get them upstairs and out of those wet things. Tia, you help Lisa, I . . .'

Lisa murmured a protest and begged feverishly for her aunt Jessica. 'Go with Lisa, Tia Sofia,' Sebastian said quietly. 'I can help Jessica.'

Jessica wanted to protest, to tell him that she was too weak now to endure the touch of his hands on her body without betraying her love—a love he did not want. She knew that now. She had seen rejection in his eyes when he turned away from her by the cellar door when she had looked at him with her heart in hers.

He took her to a room she had never seen before, richly furnished in peaches and greens.

'You will want to be alone,' he told her almost curtly. 'This was my mother's room, it is part of the suite she shared with my father. I once said that when I married my wife would always share my bed, but there are times . . .' He paused by the door. 'I am sorry about the child. I did not intend that it should happen,' and then he was depositing her on the bed, ignoring the dark smudges she was making on the silk coverlet.

The child? Did he mean . . .? But . . .

He disappeared into the bathroom, re-emerging several seconds later with a sponge and towel.

'Tia Sofia told me,' he said quietly. 'She was concerned for you and wanted me to know.'

'She may be mistaken,' Jessica told him, as a terrible pain tore at her heart. He didn't want her and he didn't want their child.

'Perhaps.' He didn't sound convinced. 'Come,

let me sponge your skin, and then I will leave you in peace. You will feel better directly.'

She would never feel better again, Jessica thought numbly as he sponged away the dirt and dust, treating her as though she were a child of Lisa's age. The warmth of the room was making her feel sleepy, soothing away the intense cold that had gripped her in the cellar.

Sebastian finished his self-imposed task and reached for the towel, and Jessica looked at him. His face seemed almost austere, and for the first time she could see the ascetic in him. 'You had a lucky escape.' He said it almost broodingly, and Jessica wondered bitterly if he had hoped that she wouldn't.

'It was lucky for us that you knew about Lisa's special place,' she told him.

His mouth tightened and he seemed about to say something, but instead he simply dried her body, then pushed back the covers. As he lifted her and slid her beneath the sheets, Jessica had a wild longing to reach up to him and beg him to stay with her, to take her in his arms and heal her aching body with the beneficence of his. But what was the point? He didn't want her; he didn't want their child. He probably wished he had never married her.

She was almost asleep when the doctor came, accompanied to her disappointment by Tia Sofia and not Sebastian. He examined her thoroughly, smiled at her and told her that she was a very brave young lady and that she had had a lucky escape.

'It is fortunate that your pregnancy is so little advanced,' he added calmly, 'otherwise . . .'

So it was true. She was carrying Sebastian's child. Tears stung her eyes and she longed for things to be different, for him to want their child as much as she did herself.

She thought later that she must have been given something to help her sleep, because she was suddenly aware of feeling oddly lightheaded, with a longing to close her eyes. When she opened them again it was morning, and the sun was dancing on the ceiling of her bedroom.

Her bedroom! She felt like a small child banished for a sin it didn't know it had committed. Why had Sebastian put her in this room? Perhaps because he could no longer endure her presence in his room, in his bed. Perhaps the fact that she carried his child reminded him too much of the past, of Manuela who he had loved as he would never love her, but he had not kept faith with Manuela. He was denying their child. It was a strangely cowardly act for so brave a man. He hadn't hesitated to risk his own life to save both hers and Lisa's.

The day dragged. She was to stay in bed for several days, Tia Sofia told her when she came to see her. Lisa's ankle was merely sprained and she too was confined to bed. Jorge and Luisa wanted to come and see her.

'And Sebastian?' Jessica asked, dry-mouthed.

'He has had to go to Seville on business,' Sofia told her, avoiding her eyes. 'He will come and see you when he comes back.' There was pity in her eyes. 'Do not distress yourself, Jessica. Think of the child you carry and let that give you hope.'

Jessica was alone when the door opened later in the afternoon and Pilar came in. As always she was dressed impeccably and expensively, her face and nails fit to grace a *Vogue* cover.

'Ah, you are awake—that is excellent,' she purred with one of the coy smiles that Jessica dreaded. 'We can have a little talk.'

'What about?' Jessica asked wearily.

'Why, Sebastian, of course, and your folly in believing you could possibly hold him. He only married you out of pity and compunction because he thought he had wronged you. You must know that?'

She did, of course, but she realised that Maria didn't like Pilar saying so. 'And now you carry his child and you believe, foolishly, that it will give you the key to his heart. It won't. His heart . . .'

'Belongs to your sister. Yes, I know,' Jessica agreed tiredly. 'But I am his wife, Pilar, and I am to have his child.'

'His wife, yet you have separate rooms,' Pilar pointed out maliciously. 'His child . . . Yes, but men can easily have children, you cannot hope to keep him because of that. You would do better to leave now, before he asks you to do so. It must be obvious to you that he doesn't want you; that your marriage was a mistake from the start. Sebastian doesn't want you—if he did why would he move you in here?' she asked scornfully. 'He is a deeply passionate and sensual man, not a man who would give his wife her own bedroom unless he was trying to tell her something. I shall leave you now,' she finished softly, sweeping towards the door, 'but think about what I have said and soon, I am sure, you will realise that I speak the truth.'

She was gone before Jessica could retaliate, leaving her with the sickening knowledge that what she had said was probably the truth. Sebastian didn't want her, and if she had any pride, any backbone, she would leave, just as soon as she was able to!

CHAPTER TEN

'JESSICA, how are you feeling now? Tia Sofia says that you are well enough to receive visitors, but that I am not to tire you out.'

Jessica smiled at Jorge. 'How is Lisa?' she asked. 'I haven't seen her yet.'

'Recuperating faster than you. Dr Bartolo told Sebastian that if you hadn't shielded her from the cold with your coat she might well have been much worse. She has a weak chest,' he explained, 'something she inherited from her mother, and if she had got badly cold it would be aggravated. On the other hand, our good doctor is very concerned about you. He says you are too pale and drawn. You do look pale.'

'I'm just a little tired. How is everyone else, Señor Alvarez and Luisa?'

'Very well, but soon their visit ends. Señor Alvarez has invited me to visit them in Argentina,' Jorge said carelessly. 'Of course, it all depends on whether Sebastian will let me go.'

'Have you told him how you feel about Luisa?' Jessica asked him.

Jorge shook his head. 'I've never known him so unapproachable,' he admitted. 'I just don't know what's got into him.'

She did, Jessica reflected. He was feeling the strain of being tied to a marriage he didn't want. Pilar was right; it would be best if she left.

Jorge was just confiding in her how much he

wanted to go to Argentina, when the door opened and Sebastian walked in. Jessica's first thought was that he looked drained and tired; her second that he was furiously, bitterly angry.

'Er . . . I'll come back and chat to you later,' Jorge muttered to her, obviously also seeing the anger in his brother's eyes.

'What was he doing here?' Sebastian demanded angrily, when Jorge had gone. 'You are supposed to be resting!'

'He came to talk to me.'

'Just to talk?' His mouth twisted aggressively. 'Did he have to sit on your bed simply to talk to you?' Jessica couldn't understand his mood. He seemed bitterly antagonistic towards Jorge, for some unknown reason. 'And what was he talking about?'

'He was telling me that Señor Alvarez had invited him to visit Argentina, and how much he wanted to go. I suspect he thought I might be able to plead his cause with you,' Jessica added with wry self-mockery.

'Dr Bartolo tells me that you are not recovering as fast as he had hoped,' he told her with an abrupt change of front. 'He believes a change of scene might be beneficial for you. Perhaps a visit to your family.'

Jessica felt as though all the breath were being squeezed out of her lungs. It was true, he did want to get rid of her.

She turned away so that he wouldn't see the pain in her eyes. '*Por Dios,*' *he* muttered savagely, 'did you not think to tell someone where you were going? Did it not occur to you that no one knew where you were? If I hadn't thought on the long drive back from Seville of the *pequeña*'s secret place, both of you could have died there!'

'Much you would have cared!' Jessica flung at him bitterly. 'Your own child, and you talk about sending her away to some convent—and not even to one of those close enough to her to soften the blow! You tell Pilar, who you must know hates her, even though she is her sister's child. Well, that isn't going to happen to my baby! Poor Lisa, she doesn't even know she is your child, but everyone else does; how can you keep the truth from her forever? Haven't you thought of her pain and disillusionment when she discovers the truth, possibly at a time when it can do her the most harm?'

'Lisa—my child?' He frowned down at her, making her feel conscious of her flushed cheeks and undoubtedly tousled hair. 'What are you talking about?' he grated. 'Lisa is not my child!'

'I know that's the polite fiction you would want to preserve, but I've been told differently. She's Manuela's child, conceived during the time of your betrothal.'

'Who told you this?'

Jessica trembled under the look of biting anger he gave her. 'I . . .'

'No matter . . . You believed it, whoever told you. You think I would actually dishonour the girl I was to have married? A virgin?'

There was so much horror in his voice that Jessica felt acute jealousy of Manuela.

'I am not talking about dishonour, Sebastián,' she said tiredly. 'You loved her and she loved you. What could be more natural . . .'

'*Dios*, you talk as though you were reading a

fairy-tale!' he snapped at her. 'And what you
say contains about as much truth. Manuela did
have a child out of wedlock and that child is
Lisa, but she is not my child.' He saw her
expression and smiled bitterly. 'You don't
believe me? I assure you it is quite true,
although no one knows the truth apart from
myself and Pilar. Perhaps I had best tell you
the whole and then there will be no more of these
hysterical accusations about my lack of feelings
towards my "child".

'Manuela's family and mine had always been
close friends, through several generations. The
idea of a marriage between us was first mooted
when we were quite small, as is our custom, and
both of us grew up knowing we were destined to
marry, although we were more like brother and
sister. The year Manuela was eighteen we were to
marry. When she was seventeen we were formally
betrothed; it was then that Manuela's father
confided to me that he had been seriously
worried by her suddenly changed behaviour.
There were wild moods, fits of tears, terrible
emotional storms that blew up out of nothing. It
was decided that she would go to South America
to spend some time with relatives over there. Her
father felt that the change would do her good. We
parted as the friends we were. If our relationship was not all that I could have hoped for
from marriage, it was pleasant and undemanding.
I would be free to make a life for myself as
long as I was discreet. There would be children.' He broke off when he saw Jessica's
expression.

'There is no need for your pity,' he told her

brusquely. 'It is an accepted code of behaviour that harms no one. While Manuela was away I prepared for our wedding. She was to return two weeks before our wedding day. I have since learned from Pilar that her father feared if she returned any sooner her bouts of hysteria might overcome her. Pilar was already married at this time and had no idea how serious Manuela's condition had become.

'She had been away eight months, but I barely recognised her when she returned. I met her at the airport, and she was swathed in black garments, her face haggard and pale. She refused to see me when I called at the house. "Wedding nerves", her mother told me.

'A week before our marriage was due to take place I received a phone call from the hospital in Seville. Manuela had been involved in a car accident and was asking for me. They gave me no hint of whether she was injured or how badly, and it was only when I got there that they told me she was not likely to live. They also told me that she was seven months pregnant, and knowing of our betrothal they had imagined that the child was mine and had called me to ask my permission to try to save its life even though they couldn't save Manuela's.

'Of course I telephoned her parents, but they refused to come to the hospital, so great was their shame. How on earth they had expected her condition to go unnoticed at the ceremony I do not know, but it seems they believed by some miracle that once we were married, everything would be all right.

'I didn't know what to do, and then, briefly,

Manuela regained consciousness. She told me her lover had been someone she had met in Argentina, someone she loved in a way that she could never love me. She knew she was going to die and begged my forgiveness, urging me to try to save the life of her child and look after it. I learned later from ... connections in South America that her lover had also been married, something he had obviously neglected to tell her, and in some ways I wonder if it was not kinder that she should have her brief moment of happiness and then oblivion before it was destroyed by the realisation that she had been deceived.

'I stayed with her until the end. She died just after Lisa was born, and I'll never forget the look on her face when she opened her eyes and saw her child. I vowed then that I would bring Lisa up as though she had been our child. I suppose it is inevitable that people should think she was mine.'

'I'm so sorry,' Jessica managed in a husky whisper. 'I should never ... You must have loved Manuela dreadfully,' she added.

'Loved her?' He looked at her incredulously. 'As a brother, yes, but as a lover—no. One selfish part of me even rejoices that we did not marry. With the benefit of hindsight I can see that there was a weakness in her—not her fault, poor child, but the result of too much marrying among cousins, too much thinning of the blood. Her hysteria, and bouts of temper ... But I am tiring you, and Dr Bartolo says that you are to rest.'

Jessica wanted to tell him that she wasn't tired. She wanted to beg him to stay, but she knew she wouldn't. Not once during their conversation had he said anything about their marriage, and she wondered if he was regretting it as much Pilar had said.

Pilar had led her to believe that he still loved Manuela, she had lied about Lisa, while according to Sebastian ... Was Pilar too tainted with her sister's weakness, was that perhaps why, in spite of the obvious suitability of it, he had not married her? She wanted him, Jessica knew that, and she would stop at nothing to get him, she acknowledged with a sudden flash of insight. Her possessiveness was almost maniacal.

Two days passed and Dr Bartolo pronounced that Jessica was well enough to get up. Sebastian as always was scrupulously polite when he saw her, which seemed to be more and more infrequently. When they did talk, it was about the factory, the designs—polite, distant conversation that tore at her heart, leaving it bruised and aching. She couldn't stay any longer, she admitted one afternoon after he had gone to inspect the vines, and she was alone in the house, Lisa and Tia Sofia were out visiting, and Jorge had taken Señor Alvarez and Luisa on a sightseeing expedition.

Only that lunchtime Sebastian had mentioned in conversation that he had been making enquiries about a flight to England for her. His aunt had looked surprised when he mentioned that she might go for a visit, and Jessica had tried to hide the hurt in her eyes that he was so anxious to get rid of her.

And he never even mentioned their child. Dr Bartolo had confirmed that she was indeed pregnant, but Sebastian had simply compressed his mouth and looked grimly distant when, falteringly, she told him that her condition was confirmed.

Perhaps now was the time to leave, she thought miserably, before the decision was forced on her. Oh, she knew Sebastian would disguise it in the guise of sending her home for a 'holiday', but they both knew that she would not be coming back. There was simply no point.

Many of her things were still in Sebastian's room, and now would be a good time to retrieve them. She was busily engaged in removing clothes from cupboards and they were on the bed in neat piles when the door was suddenly flung open. She straightened, her heart pounding, half longing and half fearing to see Sebastian. Only it wasn't Sebastian, it was Pilar, her face contorted with a rage that made fear curl unpleasantly along Jessica's spine.

'You here!' she hissed malevolently. 'I thought I told you that Sebastian didn't want you, but then the maid tells me you are in his room!'

Jessica was just about to tell her that she was simply removing her clothes when a sudden spurt of anger—and the memory of what Sebastian had told her—moved her to say lightly, 'I am his wife, Pilar. I have a perfect right to share his room, if I want to.'

'He doesn't want you,' Pilar spat positively. 'Jesu Maria, you must know that! Sebastian is a man above all else, he would not deny himself your bed and body as he has been doing these last weeks if he desired you!'

Jessica knew that it was true, but something

compelled her to stand her ground and say calmly, 'If Sebastian has been denying himself, it is for my sake, and the sake of our child,' she added softly. 'Sebastian knows that I have . . .'

'You are to have his child?'

The bitter hatred in Pilar's eyes appalled Jessica, who realised how unwise she had been to fan the flames of the other woman's resentment. Far better to have simply told the truth. Now she was alone in the room with what she was convinced was a badly deranged woman, who was advancing on her like a panther on its prey, scarlet-tipped fingers curled into talons, as though they would like to tear into her flesh and destroy the life growing within it.

'All these years I have waited for him to turn to me,' Pilar said softly, 'all these years of waiting and watching, knowing he must eventually marry for the sake of his name, and then, just when I think he will be mine, you come along . . . Well, he will be mine,' she snapped venomously. 'Manuela thought she could take him from me, and was punished for it, and I shall not let you and the brat you carry come between me and what is rightfully mine!'

She was mad—she had to be, Jessica thought shakily as she stared at the wild eyes and twisted features. But she was also dangerous, and Jessica could almost feel those fingers on her throat, gripping it, depriving her of breath.

She backed into the corner, realising too late that it was the wrong thing to do. Pilar was stalking her like a cat with its prey, a rictus smile twisting the full lips. She lunged, her hands reaching for Jessica's throat, her wildly exultant laughter filling the room.

The door was suddenly flung open and Sebastian was standing there, his jacket thrown carelessly over one shoulder, his shirt unbuttoned at the neck, tiredness lying in the shadows and hollows of his face. His expression changed as he took in the scene, alertness replacing his earlier exhaustion.

'Pilar-*Dios*, what are you about?' He gripped her arms, dragging her away from Jessica and opening the door, as he called to someone outside.

Dr Bartolo came hurrying in, his expression one of shock as he looked at Pilar and saw the murderous intent in her eyes.

'Allow me to deal with this, my friend,' he said sorrowfully to Sebastian. 'I have been afraid for a long time that . . .' He broke off as Jessica felt herself succumbing to the eddying whirls of blackness trying to suck her down.

'I'm all right,' Jessica managed to assure him. 'Just a little faint. I . . .'

'She wanted to take you from me, Sebastian!' Pilar cried bitterly. 'I told her you were mine. I . . .'

'Pilar, you must come with me,' Dr Bartolo said firmly. 'She needs specialised treatment,' he murmured in an aside to Sebastian. 'Her behaviour has troubled me for a long time, but there is a clinic I know of where they are used to cases of this kind. She has allowed her feelings for you to become obsessive.'

Pilar allowed herself to be led out of the room, and Jessica fought off the attack of faintness that had threatened her. Her legs felt weak and shaky, but when Sebastian moved towards her she fended him off, her expression unknowingly one of sharp horror.

'I am sorry about that,' he said flatly. He had his back to her, and walked across the door leading out into the courtyard. 'I should have warned you about Pilar, but she had seemed so much improved . . . She has already suffered two breakdowns; on each occasion she convinced herself that she was deeply in love with the victim of her obsession. I am sorry that you had to be involved.'

He turned round, his eyes going to the neat pile of clothes, his expression changing, darkening. 'What is this?'

'My clothes,' Jessica told him quietly. 'I was just getting them when Pilar came in. I suppose finding me here in your room was the last straw.'

'If you wish your clothes moved from my room to yours one of the maids can do it,' he told her brusquely. 'There is no need for you . . .'

'To invade your privacy?' Jessica suggested shakily. 'You needn't worry about it happening again. I'm removing my clothes, because I'm also removing myself from your life. I'm going home.'

'No!' The denial was grittily abrasive. '*Por Dios*,' Sebastian suddenly added hoarsely, crossing the room and taking her roughly in his arms. 'I can endure no more—I will not permit you to go! You are carrying my child, and I will not allow you to go.'

'But you wanted me to go,' Jessica reminded him shakily, wondering if he could feel the unsteady thud of her heart, and the quick race of her pulse. His arms felt like a haven—heaven itself, and she never wanted to leave them. She could see the faint beginnings of a beard growing along his jaw, and wanted to touch it. He smelled of the outdoors and fresh sweat, and the combination was unbearably erotic to her heightened senses.

'Because I feared something like this would happen.'

Within the circle of his arms, she raised her hand to push her hair back off her forehead, the brief gesture emphasising the gentle thrust of her breasts. Sebastian's eyes flared hotly as he studied the soft mounds, then with a savage imprecation he drew her against the hard pulsating length of him, letting her feel his arousal, his mouth moving blindly over her skin, touching and tasting, until he buried it hotly in hers, kissing her with an intensity that sapped her willpower and made her cling helplessly to him, offering herself up to whatever it was he wanted from her.

'I won't let you leave me,' he muttered throatily against her skin. 'You are mine, Jessica, and mine alone. *Dios*, the torment I have suffered seeing you smile at my brother, my aunt—anyone but me! You cannot know how I have longed to see you look at me with love, how I have hungered for you to want me as I want you—not simply for the pleasure our bodies find in one another, but with your heart and soul!'

She was unbearably moved, unable to deny the conviction in his voice, the emotion in his eyes as they searched her face as though willing a response.

'You love me?' Jessica asked uncertainly, still not fully able to accept.

'Do you doubt it?' He smoothed her hair back off her forehead, and she could feel the heated shudder of his body as she touched him. 'I wanted you from the first,' he told her softly. 'I hated you at the same time because of what you were. Or what I thought you were.'

'I thought you despised me,' Jessica told him. 'You were so cold, so distant.'

'Because I daren't let myself be anything else. All the time I was giving myself reasons why I shouldn't, all I wanted to do was to take you in my arms and make you admit that no man could give you the pleasure I could. I hated Jorge because he had been your lover, and when you threatened to stay in Seville and see him. I couldn't understand why he had stopped wanting you. I thought if he saw you again, he would do . . .'

'And so you concocted that tale about needing a designer to save him from me,' Jessica supplied dryly.

Sebastian smiled grimly. 'Nearly right, only it was because I wanted to keep you away from him and with me,' he supplemented. 'And then he arrived and my whole world was turned upside down. You weren't the girl he had met, you were someone else; someone about whom I knew nothing. Someone who might have a lover or a boy-friend in the background whose claims on you I couldn't destroy. And then Jorge gave me the perfect weapon. People were talking about us, he told me. He was concerned for you. I knew my aunt and Pilar intended to come and see you. I must admit I hadn't quite intended that we should be discovered as we were . . . some things cannot be controlled,' he added with a wry mockery that brought vivid colour to her skin, 'and you were so sweetly responsive I forgot why I had come to your room and remembered only how much I wanted you ... loved you,' he amended softly, 'because by then I did, although I was loath to admit it even to myself.'

'But when you married me you were so distant I thought you hated me!'

He cupped her face and looked at her sombrely. 'Why didn't you tell me you were a virgin? Was it to punish me, to make me suffer?'

Jessica didn't understand what he meant.

'I tried to,' she told him huskily, 'in the car on the way back to the *hacienda*, but you told me how relieved you were that I didn't need "initiating" and after that I just couldn't ...'

'And so instead you make me suffer a thousand torments, hating myself for what I have done to you. It was bad enough when I simply thought I was forcing you into a marriage you didn't want. There was desire between us and I hoped that in time it might grow to something else. When I discovered that not only had I robbed you of your freedom, but that I had also taken from you the right to give your body and sweet innocence to the lover of your choice, I hated and despised myself ...'

'You were so cold,' Jessica whispered, 'so distant, and so hateful.'

'Because it was the only way I could stop myself from taking you in my arms and making love to you again and again,' Sebastian told her whimsically. 'I wanted you so much, I had to erect a barrier between us for your sake. I wanted to get down on my knees and beg your forgiveness, kiss every inch of your beautiful, precious body and promise you that never again would it know pain, but to do so would be to inflict my desire and love on you again, and I told myself that was something I would never do.

'We both know how long my resolve lasted,' he added wryly, adding with a frankness that half shocked her, 'Your sweet cries of pleasure on that second occasion have haunted my nights like a siren song ever since.'

'You made me sleep on my own,' Jessica accused, still not daring to believe that it was true and that he loved her.

He smothered a groan. 'My sweet love, it was torture, but I had no alternative. I had promised myself that I would set you free, that it was wrong of me to hold you to our marriage. I couldn't forgive myself for taking your innocence when you didn't love me, and when I discovered you were to have my child . . .'

'You were so cold towards me I thought you didn't want it,' Jessica interrupted bleakly. 'Then Pilar came and told me that you wanted me to leave, and . . .'

'And you already believed that I had turned my back on my daughter,' he finished for her. 'Oh, Jessica, I can't tell you what it meant to me to think you carried my child! I longed fiercely to keep you here with me, but I couldn't do it. I couldn't hold you on so fragile a thread. I'm a proud man, as you have so often said, and my pride would not allow me to constrain my wife to stay with me only for the sake of our child.'

'But if she loved you . . .'

He cupped her chin, his eyes dark with emotion. 'If she loved me—if you loved me,' he corrected huskily, 'I would never let her go. When I saw that building and knew you were in it . . . If you had died then life would have had no meaning for me,' he told her simply.

'You risked your life for us,' Jessica said softly. 'I . . .'

'Do you think I would have let anyone else near you?' he demanded with a ferocity that surprised her. 'When everything a man holds of value in his life is in danger of course he trusts no one but himself to remove that danger. When you told me to take Lisa, even though I knew you were right, you'll never know what it cost me to go, leaving you there, possibly facing death.'

'And you'll never know how I felt, seeing you disappear,' Jessica told him softly, 'wanting you so badly . . . and then you were so cold, putting me in that bedroom when all I wanted was the warmth of your arms, your . . .'

'My . . .?' he questioned teasingly. 'Go on, *querida*, you are just about to get to the interesting bit, I think?'

'Your . . . body against mine,' Jessica admitted hesitantly, laughing at her own shyness. 'Oh, Sebastian,' she sighed ecstatically, 'I fell in love with you almost straight away, despite all those dreadful things you said to me!'

She frowned as Sebastian suddenly released her, picking up the piles of clothes from the bed and depositing them on a chair.

'What are you doing?' she asked anxiously. 'Sebastian . . .'

'I thought you wanted to be in my arms,' he

reminded her with a slow smile, 'to feel my body against yours? Is that not right, *querida*?'

'Oh, but . . .' She tried to look scandalised and failed, laughing when he took her in his arms and said wryly,

'What is the matter? Is it not permissible for a man to make love to his wife in the afternoon?'

'I . . .'

He nibbled the delicate cord of her throat, sending tremors of pleasure coursing over her. 'Why else do you think we have the *siesta*, *amada*?' he questioned softly. 'It is for children to rest, and for their *mamás* and *papás* to make love.'

His fingers reached for her zip, pressing her against the taut length of his body, and the sudden urgency of the desire flooding through her made her expel her breath in brief shock.

'I love you,' Sebastian murmured smokily as her dress slid to the floor.

As he lifted her and carried her towards their bed Jessica wondered hazily if that first Rosalinda had known this heady, enveloping pleasure; this depth and intensity of love and need for her proud knight. Possibly she had, she thought lazily as Sebastian drew her against him, his fingers playing lightly against her spine, his mouth teasing her skin. Certainly if he was anything like his present-day descendant, she must have done!

Harlequin® Plus

A WORD ABOUT THE AUTHOR

Born in Preston, a small city north of Liverpool, Penny Jordan was constantly in trouble as a schoolgirl because of her inability to stop daydreaming—the first sign of possible talent as a writer! When she was not daydreaming, she spent most of her spare time curled up somewhere with a book. Early in her teens, she was introduced to romance novels and became an avid reader, but at the time it didn't occur to her to try to write one herself.

That changed when she entered her thirties and felt an urge to make a mark in the world by means of her own talent. She had many false starts—lots of "great" ideas ended up in the wastepaper basket. But finally the day came when Penny completed her first book-length manuscript. And, to her utter amazement, it wasn't long before the novel was accepted for publication.

Now she has received many letters of acceptance for her books, and every letter brings the thrill of knowing that the stories on which she has worked so hard will reach the readers for whom each is lovingly written.

ROBERTA LEIGH

A specially designed collection of six exciting love stories by one of the world's favorite romance writers—Roberta Leigh, author of more than 60 bestselling novels!

1 **Love in Store**   4 **The Savage Aristocrat**
2 **Night of Love**   5 **The Facts of Love**
3 **Flower of the Desert** 6 **Too Young to Love**

Available now wherever paperback books are sold, or available through Harlequin Reader Service. Simply complete and mail the coupon below.

Harlequin Reader Service

In the U.S.
P.O. Box 52040
Phoenix, AZ 85072-9988

In Canada
649 Ontario Street
Stratford, Ontario N5A 6W2

Please send me the following editions of the Harlequin Roberta Leigh Collector's Editions. I am enclosing my check or money order for $1.95 for each copy ordered, plus 75¢ to cover postage and handling.

☐ 1   ☐ 2   ☐ 3   ☐ 4   ☐ 5   ☐ 6

Number of books checked_____ @ $1.95 each = $_____

N.Y. state and Ariz. residents add appropriate sales tax $_____

Postage and handling $___.75___

                                               TOTAL $_____

I enclose_____

(Please send check or money order. We cannot be responsible for cash sent through the mail.) Price subject to change without notice.

NAME_____

(Please Print)

ADDRESS_____ APT. NO._____

CITY_____

STATE/PROV._____ ZIP/POSTAL CODE_____

Offer expires April 30, 1984   31056000000